Dead in the Water

Bucket List Mysteries

S.C. Merritt

Published by Sweet Southern Reads Publishing, 2021.

This is a work of fiction. Similarities to real people, places, or events are entirely coincidental.

DEAD IN THE WATER

First edition. July 27, 2021.

Copyright © 2021 S.C. Merritt.

Written by S.C. Merritt.

1

I JOLTED AT THE EAR-splitting sound of the smoke alarm blaring from the kitchen.

"My biscuits!!" Slamming the computer chair into the side of the bed, I jumped up from my desk and tore out of my tiny bedroom for the kitchen. Angus, my Scottish Terrier, leapt from his snoozing place on the bed and ran after me.

Picking up the nearest potholder, I took the pan of scorched biscuits out of the oven, practically throwing it onto the top of the stove. Smoke billowed from the open oven door. Grabbing a broom out of the pantry, I poked at the smoke alarm until it finally stopped screeching.

"Maisie Mitchell! Why do you always do that?" I chided myself. Coughing, I looked down at Angus who looked back innocently at me and wagged his tail. "Angus, I know better than to sit down to work on the blog when I have food in the oven." Frustrated with myself, I opened the kitchen door to the patio and began fanning the air with a paper plate to chase out the smoke. I had taken perfect pictures of my prep work before the biscuits went into the oven, but now I would have to make another batch just to get the after pictures I needed for this week's blog post. There would barely be enough time to get a new batch done before my water aerobics class.

I took the freshly washed bowl I'd used just an hour earlier and got to work mixing up a new batch. After adding all the ingredients, I plopped the dough out onto my floured countertop. Giving it a few good smacks with my fist like my Granny used to do, I rolled it out to just the right thickness for cutting. I used the old biscuit cutter, one of the few items I'd kept from the restaurant, and began cutting the perfect circles of dough, placing them on the baking sheet. This time I made sure to set the oven timer as soon as the pan went into the oven and started cleaning up the kitchen for the second time.

Wiping my hands on my apron, I checked the countertop area to make sure it was clean and photo-ready as soon as the biscuits came out. I wanted to get a good shot with the Florida sunlight glistening off the melting butter while they were still hot out of the oven. I heard a knock at the door, and Angus took off like a cartoon dog, sliding sideways on the wood floor as he rounded the corner to the front entryway. I glanced at the timer and then hurried to the front door.

"Hi, Dot." I swung open the door just as the timer sounded. "Come on in. I'm almost done." I hurried back to the kitchen as my friend bent down to give Angus a scratch on the head.

"I thought you would've been done with those ages ago." Dot stopped short and sniffed the lingering smokiness in the air, her eyes landing on the trash bin. "Second batch, huh?"

"Oh, you hush! You know how easy it is for me to get sidetracked when I leave the room with food in the oven." I carefully brushed the melted butter across the tops of the hot biscuits and aimed the camera. Click. "Perfect!" Satisfied with the pictures for the blog, I took a couple of plates from the cabinet. "Now, how about an afternoon treat?"

Dot licked her lips at the sight of the pan of buttery goodness. Opening the refrigerator, she pulled out a jar of my homemade peach preserves and grabbed a knife. "You don't have to ask me twice! I'm going to need a couple of extra laps around the pool after our class to work this off."

Donna Pinetta was one of the newest residents at Palm Gardens, relocating to Florida after retiring from the police department in Chicago. After a couple of months, I began calling her Dot, because she was always in the middle of everything. Plus, I thought it sounded more southern, but Dot was anything but southern. Hot-blooded Italian was more of an accurate description. We were basically total opposites, but Dot had a huge heart and a determination to get things done, and I loved that about her.

"Now aren't you glad you let Connie talk you into all of this?" she said referring to my recent foray into the computer age. "I know I've said this before, but I'm really proud of you for taking this huge step. You aced the computer class at the community college and now you have your own blog!" She smiled from ear to ear.

"I certainly never pictured myself doing anything like this," I said swiping the sweat off my forehead with the back of my wrist. "I've spent the majority of my adult life in a kitchen. I never saw any reason for me to learn all that computer stuff. Eddie handled all the books for the restaurant."

"I'm sure you could've done it, if you'd given yourself a chance," she said.

"I'm sure I could, but after he died, I just didn't see how I could keep the restaurant going without him. The truth is, I really didn't want to. When I made the decision to sell it, our son, Peter, and his family tried to convince me to come live with them in upstate New York, but I was never a fan of snow and cold weather."

Dot laughed. "I can relate to that. Growing up in Chicago, I was ready for some rest and relaxation in the warm, Florida sunshine, too."

"Exactly! Or at least that's what I thought. It didn't take long to realize that I really missed having someone to cook for."

"Enter Connie and her cooking class idea, right?

"Yep. She saw a chance to offer something fun to the residents here, but I think she knew that I needed it, too. When the cooking class became so popular that she had to start filming it for the website, that's when she got the idea of a food blog."

"And the rest, they say, is history! Maisie's Southern Comfort is doing great!" She clapped her hands. "How many followers do you have now? Two thousand?"

I nodded. "I guess that's pretty good for a beginner. I still can't believe that many people care about what I cook," I said, shaking my head.

"Mmmm, these are so good," Dot groaned in delight. "You should do this for a living," she teased.

"Been there. Done that." I laughed and threw a kitchen towel in her direction which she adeptly dodged. "Would you be a dear and cover the rest of these with foil while I change into my swimsuit? I'm sure we'll be ready for another snack after class."

"Which means I'll have to run an extra mile around the complex. Are you trying to kill me?" Dot laughed, tearing off a sheet to cover the pan. One of the ways we weren't even remotely alike was in the area of fitness. Dot was in perfect shape from her days on the force and planned to stay that way. She even held a black belt in karate. I, on the other hand, had never been one for a lot of formal exercising. Running all day long, sweating off the calories in a hot kitchen had been more than enough for me. But lately I'd begun to notice, since I wasn't in the restaurant any longer, the pounds were creeping up on me. Dot had recently taken it upon herself to enroll us both in a new water aerobics class being offered at the Rec Center indoor pool. I had reluctantly agreed and was reserving judgement until at least after our first session.

I hurried to the bedroom and changed into my swimsuit, grabbed my pool bag, and returned to the kitchen. "Angus, you be a good boy while we're out." I bent down and looked into the Scottie's beady, black eyes. "No nosing in the trash, okay?"

"Is he still doing that?" Dot asked. "Why don't you let me give him some obedience classes? I'll have him trained just like Magnum." Magnum was Dot's German Shepherd. He was a former police dog, retired from the same precinct on the same day. Dot said it was a sign that they should enjoy retirement together and I had to agree. They were inseparable.

"Maybe. I'll think about it. Sometimes when dogs are professionally trained, they seem to lose some of their...I don't know...cuddliness. I've read that to stay in control, you can never give in to them. I think I'd rather clean up a mess every once in a while, and still get to spoil my little buddy."

Dot shrugged. "Suit yourself. Just remember that statement the next time you're cleaning mustard and ketchup stains from a three-day-old hot dog out of your carpet."

2

THE REC CENTER WAS only a block away, so the walk was a good way to get our blood pumping before we started exercising. Palm Gardens was, according to their website, an "exciting lifestyle community for active seniors," and I'd been very happy here from the first day I'd moved in.

We chatted and enjoyed the sun as we strolled down the sidewalk, passing house after house of friends, and waving to a few who happened to be out in their yards. As we crossed the street to the other side, I heard a friendly voice.

"Afternoon, ladies!" Stanley Taylor was headed our way up ahead. "Where are y'all off to?" There were three sections of Palm Gardens: The Cottages, The Cabanas, and The Villas. Stanley was the head of maintenance for the cottage side of the community, which is where both Dot and I lived. The homes in our section were small, ranch patio homes. They were just the right size for one or two people. Stanley was leaving one of the homes with a bag of tools in one hand and a broken toilet seat in the other. His gray work shirt was damp with the Florida humidity and spotted with random stains, evidence of his hard work.

"Water aerobics," Dot called back. "Gotta keep in peak condition. I didn't work this hard for the last thirty-five years just to let it all go to pot, now." She patted her flat stomach.

I self-consciously wrapped my cover-up even further around my ample midsection and tugged it down in the back. Thirty-five years of taste-testing biscuits and gravy looked a lot different in a swimsuit than her black belt in karate. "Dot seems to think I could use a little exercise." I laughed, knowing Dot was absolutely right. "I'm afraid I can't keep up with her, but maybe I can do as well as some of the others."

"You'll do fine! Good exercise and a hard day's work are the keys to staying young," he smiled. "Have a good workout! Don't you let that creep Mason make any inappropriate moves on you ladies," he said as he passed us on the sidewalk.

Stopping in our tracks, we turned, and Dot called after Stanley.

"Why would you say that? Have you heard complaints from residents?" she asked, her eyebrows arched.

"Just rumors." A frown wrinkled Stanley's brow as he scratched his gray-stubbled chin and took a couple of steps back toward us. "All the same, you let me know if it happens and I'll nip it in the bud. I have plenty of things in this tool bag that would put a crimp in his style." He lifted the bag up. "I don't like that guy. Mark my words, he's nothing but trouble."

We nodded and resumed the trek towards the pool and Stanley went on his way. Mason Jacobs was a new staff member at Palm Gardens. He had taken over as Recreation Manager when Polly Morgan moved to Orlando a little over three months ago.

"What do you make of that?" I asked. "I've only seen Mason in passing a few times, but he seemed okay to me."

"I haven't noticed anything, but you can bet my radar will be up from now on." Dot frowned and shook her head. "I've worked too many cases of young men preying on older women to cheat them out of their life savings. That's just the lowest of the low."

We continued our walk, picking up the pace since stopping to talk with Stanley had thrown us a little behind. By the time we reached the Rec Center, I noticed that Dot had barely broken a sweat while I was sucking wind like a vacuum cleaner. It was becoming painfully clear that I needed this class more than she did. As we headed to the locker room to drop off our bags, we heard raised voices coming from inside.

"I don't care if you were Miss Florida. That was umpteen years ago," a voice threatened. "You keep your hands off him. He's not the least bit interested in you, you...cougar!"

"At least I haven't let myself go like *some* people," the other voice said. "I still have my hourglass figure."

"Sure, you do, honey, but all the sand has run to the bottom half." The door flew open, and Fiona Scranton stopped in her tracks to keep from walking straight into us. "Oh, hello, ladies." She flushed with embarrassment. "Excuse me. I'll see you in the water." She hurried past us and kept walking, letting the door bang shut behind her.

I eased the locker room door open and peeked in. Joan Trulove was admiring herself in a mirror and touching up her lipstick. "Hi, Joan," I said, causing her to jump and smear lipstick all the way down onto her chin.

"Look what you made me do!" she screeched. She grabbed a tissue and began scrubbing it off.

"I'm sorry," I apologized and heard Dot snort behind me. "But why on earth do you bother wearing makeup into the pool?"

Joan let out a dramatic sigh. "People expect me to look put together constantly. It gets bothersome, but I suppose the public has a right to expect their beauty queens to live up to a certain standard." She looked me and Dot up and down. "I do wish I could be more like you ladies and not be so concerned about making a good impression." She slung her towel over her shoulder and walked out. We stared after her in stunned silence.

"I'm not sure if that was intended as a backhanded compliment or not," I said, shaking my head.

"Well, the one and only time I wore makeup was when I was a bridesmaid in my sister's wedding thirty years ago, so I'm not even sure what she's talking about," Dot said, slipping her feet into her flip flops. "I believe in keeping life simple." Her beautiful, olive skin was a testament to her Italian heritage.

"Working in a hot kitchen day in and day out, made me give up on makeup a long time ago, too. I haven't worn a lick of makeup in years, and I'll be switched if I'd wear it for anybody now." I shook my head. "No, ma'am. Not at my age."

Dot placed her bag and belongings in one of the lockers and closed the door, checking to make sure it locked. "Who's Joan trying to impress, anyway? Just a bunch of old coots around here. Wouldn't take much to impress any of them."

"Well, Fiona must think she's after somebody. Her claws came out, and I thought we were about to see a cat fight for sure. I've never seen her that upset. She's usually the sweetest thing." I closed the door on my locker and grabbed my towel.

We headed toward the indoor pool area and joined the rest of the class. I was hoping it would be ladies only so I wouldn't feel so self-conscious, but I was out of luck. Luther Bodkins was already in the water and right beside him was Pete Kowalski splashing up a storm. There were several other women and, of course, Fiona and Joan. Fiona was already in the water, but Joan had conveniently lingered by the pool chair to be the last to enter the pool. She slowly removed her cover-up and kicked off her kitten heels in a production worthy of an Academy Award. Luther and Pete may or may not have had a coronary in the water, but it was obvious whose benefit the show was for. Mason Jacobs sat on the edge of the pool with his clipboard, calling out names. His tanned, muscular body and sun-kissed blonde hair made every female take a second look—and he knew it. After Joan slithered into the water, he hopped off the side and began the class.

3

FEELING REJUVENATED from the exercise, I toweled my curly hair and twisted it up into a sloppy top knot while Dot did her extra laps. "I'll be right back, Dot. I'm gonna grab us some water from the Snack Shack," I called as she did a flip at the other end of the pool. I slid my feet into my sandals and padded the short walk to the complex office. The Snack Shack was a little room in the office which was next door to the Rec Center. It was late in the day, but I hoped it would still be open. I breathed in the fresh air as I entered the breezeway connecting the two buildings, clearing my lungs of the muggy, indoor pool air. I opened the door to the office and was disappointed to find it empty. Emily, the receptionist, must have already left for the day. I turned to leave when I heard voices coming from the back. Maybe Connie was still there. She wouldn't mind if I grabbed two bottles of water.

"Come on, Connie. You know you want it," a familiar male voice said. "Quit fighting it. We're perfect for each other."

"Get your slimy hands off me, Mason. I told you, I'm not interested. If you don't leave me alone, I'll tell my husband and you'll wish you'd never started this ridiculous mess," Connie said. "I mean it, Mason!" Her voice grew louder.

I started down the hall to see if Connie needed help. I heard papers rustling and the sound of a struggle, then, *smack!*

The unmistakable sound of a well-deserved slap across the face. Just as I reached for the doorknob, the door swung open and Mason Jacobs stomped past me, hair still wet from the pool and holding his head back, nursing a bloody nose. I rushed past him into the room.

"Connie, are you alright?" I bent down to help her gather papers off the floor. "I couldn't help but hear."

"Yes, I'm fine," she said straightening her blouse. "He's such a jerk. No matter how many times I tell him that I'm happily married, he just won't let it go." Connie was a petite redhead. Her fashionable eyeglass frames changed daily to coordinate with her outfits. She oozed style, but the girl had brains, too. Smart as a whip. She had done wonders for the complex since she took over as manager.

"I'm sorry. I just came in to see if I could get two bottles of water. Do you mind?"

"Not at all. I was just about to leave." She picked up her purse and cell phone and closed the door behind us as we headed back up front.

"Stanley mentioned something to me and Dot this afternoon on our way to aerobics about hearing some rumors about Mason. This must've been what he was talking about. He certainly didn't try to hide the fact that he doesn't like Mason at all."

She frowned. "Stanley has mentioned it to me, too. I hired Mason on the recommendation of a friend. I should have done more checking into his background. Last week I found out that he lost his last two jobs for this very reason. Unwanted advances toward residents. Any age seems to do. He's not picky!"

"What do you mean?"

"His last job was at a nursing home!"

"Oh my!" My hand flew to my mouth. "Either he has a bad problem, or he has ulterior motives for making up to these women."

"Last week I caught him in my office, going through residents' private information. After I fill out all the paperwork and make sure I cover all the legal bases in his files, I'm going to fire him. I just hope he doesn't cause trouble." She handed me the bottles of water. "On the house. Thanks again, Maisie."

I waved and headed back to the Rec Center where Dot was waiting just outside the front entrance.

"What took you so long? I was about to give up and head back to the house without you."

I tossed Dot a bottle and, on the walk home, I told her what happened between Mason and Connie and about the things that Connie had discovered about Mason's past employment.

"I'm telling you, Maisie. I've seen this before." She shook her head in dismay. "Connie had better get rid of him and soon!"

"How old do you think Mason is? Maybe thirty?" I asked. "I can understand him being interested in Connie. She's young and pretty, but what could he possibly want with women our age? Especially Fiona. She has to be at least sixty-five or seventy. Why would he do that? Is this just a game to him? Does he just get his kicks from seeing women fight over him?"

"Oh, I have a feeling it's more than a game to Mason. I'm afraid he's only after one kind of relationship—cash and carry."

"That conversation we heard in the locker room between Fiona and Joan is beginning to make more sense," I said. "Do you think Mason is leading both of them on?"

"You may be right."

As I unlocked the door to the house, we were greeted by a little black furball begging for kisses. "Hello, Angus. Yes, I know it's your dinnertime," I cooed as I scooped food into his bowl and gave him fresh water.

"Mason knows exactly what he's doing," Dot continued, taking a seat at the kitchen table. "You know Fiona is loaded. Her husband left her a fortune."

"You're kidding me!" I exclaimed. I stepped into the laundry room and emptying my pool bag, hung up my wet towel and swimsuit.

"You've seen her wear all that jewelry to our formal dinner nights, haven't you?" Dot talked a little louder so I could hear her until I returned to the kitchen.

"Sure, but I thought that was all just imitation. Do you mean that's all real?" I thought back to last Valentine's Day when the complex sponsored a black-tie dinner party in the Rec Center for all the residents. Fiona had worn a black sequined gown with a necklace and earrings full of rubies and diamonds.

"Yes, it's the real thing. She asked me to come by and give her some advice on the best way to keep it safe. She keeps it all in a combination safe in her master closet."

I peeled the foil back from the top of the biscuit pan. "Wow. This calls for another biscuit." I grabbed two from the pan and warmed them in the microwave for a few seconds. Then after splitting them in half, I layered sliced strawberries in the middle and topped them with whipped cream. I handed Dot a fork and we dug in.

"Goodness, this is delicious! I've never thought to use a biscuit for strawberry shortcake." Dot took another bite.

"My momma always did this when we didn't have money for cake. We always had leftover biscuits on hand." I poured us both a glass of tea and slid one over to Dot.

"What about Joan?" Dot mumbled around a mouthful of strawberries. "Do you think Mason's after her or is it the other way around?"

"Joan really is a hard one to figure out. I think she's one of the youngest residents here. I guarantee you that she's barely old enough to qualify to live in Palm Gardens, so I'm not sure why she chose to buy a cottage here." I took my first bite and closed my eyes in delight. "She strikes me more as the type who would want to live in the middle of the big city. Glitz and glamour and movie premieres and such with all her beauty pageant friends." I shrugged. "I don't know; it just seems odd to me."

"Well, she lives and breathes the stuff, that's for sure. I've never been in a conversation with her when she didn't mention her pageant titles. She's always so condescending to everyone. Like no one measures up to her standards." Dot put her dishes in the sink and picked up her pool bag. "I need to get going. It's past Magnum's dinnertime and if I'm any later he won't speak to me for a week."

We said our goodbyes and I locked the door behind her, then headed for a long, hot bath. Water aerobics may not seem strenuous while you're doing it, but my muscles were screaming at me now. I turned on some music and stepped carefully into the lavender-scented bath water. Letting out a slow, relaxing breath, I sank into the bubbles. I tried to clear my mind of everything and just relax, but I kept hearing Stanley's words over and over in my head. *"Mark my words. He's nothing but trouble. Nothing but trouble."*

4

"IT'S GOING TO TAKE more than a hot shower and some ibuprofen to help these aching muscles, Angus," I said as I threw off the covers. My body wanted to crawl back into the bed and sleep another hour, but my mind knew I should get up and get moving. I wiggled my feet into my flamingo slippers and slipped into the kitchen to let Angus out for his morning business. I put on a pot of coffee to brew and scooped his breakfast into his dish. Scratching at the back door to let me know that he was ready to eat, I let him back in and while I waited on the coffee, I flipped open my Bible for my morning devotion.

"How sweet are your words to my taste, sweeter than honey to my mouth." Psalm 119:103

This time of the day was the most peaceful, and meditating on a scripture really was the best way to start my day, but I had to admit, I loved sleeping in. It was a work in progress. A knock roused me from my quiet time.

Dot and Magnum stood at the door, annoyingly vivacious and energetic.

"Good morning, Maisie!" she chirped. "I saw your light on. I hope it's not too early for you."

"Mornin', Dot. Mornin', Magnum. Not at all. Come on in," I said trying not to spill my coffee as I bent to stroke the top of the majestic dog's head. "How about a cup of coffee?"

"Love one," Dot walked in and closed the door behind them. She and Magnum followed me to the kitchen table and took a seat. Angus barked and danced circles around Magnum, who completely ignored him.

I handed her a mug of the steaming brew and joined her at the table. "I'm assuming you and Magnum have already been out for your run around the lake this morning?" Vista Lake was at the center of the Palm Gardens community and the paved path that ran around the lake was just the right distance for a good run, or at least that's what Dot said.

Dot nodded as she blew across the top of her coffee and took a sip. "Yep! And do I have some juicy news for you!"

I cocked an eyebrow. "Do tell!"

"Magnum and I were headed toward the lake trail and as we passed by the Rec Center, I heard raised voices. Being the nosy detective that I am, I stepped behind a bush and waited to see who it was."

"Of course, you did. Once a cop, always a cop." I grinned.

"Well, I've never seen him, but I'm pretty sure it was Brad Lee. After you told me about that incident last night in Connie's office, it had to be him. He said 'This is your last warning, Jacobs. If I find out you've made another pass at my wife, I'll bash your skull in.' Then he ran out of the Rec Center, got into a black sedan and squealed tires out of the parking lot."

"Connie must have told him what happened with Mason. Brad must have been pretty mad to hunt Mason down at this time of morning. I hope Mason will back off before something really bad happens. He's just asking for trouble." Angus stood beside the back door and stared at me. He wasn't much of a whiner when he wanted to go out, but he could stare a hole into my soul. I let both dogs out for a little sniff around the yard and sat back down.

"There's more," Dot continued, taking a sip of her coffee. "After I run each morning, I stop by the Rec Center to lift a few weights before heading home for breakfast. I was just finishing the leg press when Luther and Pete came in. The sight of those two decked out in spandex workout shorts and white muscle shirts—well, let's just say I had to pinch my eyes shut to keep from gawking. I certainly didn't want those two to think I was ogling them."

"Luther and Pete working out? I'm sure that's a sight you can't unsee." I laughed.

"I commented that it was the first time I'd seen them in the gym, and they said they were working on their physiques so that when Mason dumps Joan and Fiona and moves on to younger pastures, they could be there to boost the girls' egos."

"I'm sure they aren't fond of Mason any more than Stanley is. The competition for the men around here is already tough enough. It seems to me that there are a lot more single men than women living here."

"I asked them what they thought about the 'love triangle,'" Dot admitted.

"I'm sure they had no shortage of opinion on that subject."

"Luther said they'd been meaning to talk to me about how concerned they are for Fiona. She seems to be really taken in by Mason's charms. He's been wining and dining her for weeks now, and Fiona said he's even mentioned marriage."

"Marriage! Surely it hasn't gone that far." My eyes widened.

"They think he's up to no good and is only after her money and I have to say, I agree with them." A frown creased Dot's forehead as she took another drink of coffee. "I asked them to keep their eyes and ears open and report back to me if they hear anything else."

"Dot, we have to do something. Fiona's too nice a lady to get taken in by that charlatan. It has to be obvious that he's just after her fortune."

"Sure, to us it's a no-brainer. Now, how do we convince Fiona of that without hurting her feelings?" Dot stared into her cup. "What about Joan? Maybe he'll lose interest in Fiona if Joan gets her claws into him."

"Joan loves Joan," I said. "She thinks every man should be fawning all over her and her crown. For every drop of sweetness in Fiona, there's a drop of vinegar in Joan."

Dot nodded. "I've never seen someone so self-absorbed. It's like she didn't exist before that pageant. It's really pretty sad. Her whole life is wrapped up in her identity as Miss Florida." Dot's stomach made a rumbling sound. "I'm starving. What do you think about joining me for breakfast at Keke's? They have wonderful omelets and the absolute best fried potatoes and onions."

I cocked an eyebrow. "The best, huh?" I feigned offense.

"Besides yours, of course." Dot laughed.

"Anything to keep from heating up this kitchen today. It's gonna be a scorcher. Maybe we could go to the pool afterwards. My pasty complexion could use a little Vitamin D."

"That's not a bad idea," Dot agreed. "We might just run into Fiona. Maybe we could get her to open up about her plans with Mason."

"Meet me at my house in twenty minutes," she said. "And don't forget Angus!" She and Magnum closed the door behind them.

I hurried to the back and grabbed a quick shower. As I dried my hair, I couldn't help but think about the comments by Joan. Should I make more of an effort to look put together all the time? I studied the laugh lines and the dark circles underneath my eyes. Maybe a little concealer once in a while wouldn't hurt. But not before breakfast, I decided. I brushed my teeth and smiled in the mirror. *That's enough primping for one morning.*

I grabbed Angus' leash from the hook near the door and snapped it to his collar. One of the reasons we loved Keke's so much, aside from the wonderful food, was the outdoor seating. It was a nice, shaded area and they welcomed dogs on the patio.

"You have to be a good boy while we eat, Angus," I said, bending down and looking directly into his black eyes. "I'll take along some treats and your collapsible water bowl." He wagged his little tail and barked in what I hoped was agreement. I tucked the items in my bag, and we headed out the door to Dot's house.

I was relieved that Dot offered to drive. I wasn't a fan of dog hair in my car and German Shepherds shed so much more than terriers. She did her best to keep him groomed and brushed, but it's just the nature of the breed.

The boys were exceptionally well-behaved during breakfast. Angus must have taken me seriously. Either that, or he was bored to death since Magnum continued to act like he didn't exist. He laid down in the warm sun and took a nap, while Magnum sat regally, head held high, and watched passersby.

"Yum, this was perfect," I said, folding my napkin neatly and leaning back in my chair. "Thanks for suggesting it. Now what are we going to do about Fiona and that sleazeball, Mason?"

"Sleazeball is right." Dot relaxed back into her chair, turning her face up to soak in the warmth of the sun. "I'm not sure what the solution is. Fiona is a grown woman. We can't very well forbid her to go out with Mason. I'm afraid her heart's going to get broken either way."

"Better a broken heart than an empty bank account," I reasoned. "Maybe we could figure out a way to push Joan and Mason together. You know, orchestrate opportunities for them to be in the same place, encourage her every chance we get. Tell her how cute he is and how we get the feeling he's been noticing her."

"Wow, you really have thought this out." Dot finished off her orange juice. She placed the glass down on the table and drew in a sharp breath. "Well, well, well...would you speak of the devil."

5

I FOLLOWED DOT'S GAZE toward a table on the other side of the patio where a man sat, wearing a tropical print shirt and a baseball cap. Blond hair sprouted out from underneath the cap. He was seated with his back to us, but there was no mistaking the person on the other side of the table. "I'm pretty sure that's Mason, alright. And he's with Emily."

Emily Potter was Connie's new administrative assistant. Not only was she beautiful, but she was much closer to Mason's age.

Dot squinted, trying to make it less obvious that she was staring at them. "I've never seen someone so brazen about courting multiple women at the same time!"

"If you ask me, that guy's just begging for trouble. You know the old saying about a woman scorned. At least Emily is more in line with his age." I watched Emily get up from the table, flash Mason one last smile and walk towards the parking lot. "If he's involved with Emily, too, then it complicates the Fiona situation even more."

"Maybe we should just go directly to the root of the problem. Why don't we have a little chat." Dot put on her sunglasses, grabbed Magnum's leash, and scooted her chair back from the table, then stopped and sat back down.

"What's the matter?" I asked slipping my glasses on as well. "Aren't we going over?"

Dot turned her back to Mason and shielded the side of her face with her hand.

I glanced toward the parking lot and saw Joan approaching. Even in the oversized, floppy sun hat and huge, designer sunglasses, that walk was unmistakable. We tried to look as inconspicuous as possible, turning our faces away as Joan sashayed right past us to join Mason at his table.

"Maybe we won't have to worry about pushing Joan and Mason together after all," I said, gathering Angus up into my lap so he wouldn't draw attention with an ill-timed bark. "Looks like Joan is turning up the heat."

We sat in silence and watched the couple, trying to make out the topic of conversation by reading their lips.

"Is it just me, or does Joan look anxious to you?" Dot observed. "I've been on a lot of stakeouts where I had to rely on body language, and she looks really nervous."

"Hmmm...maybe she's not as self-confident as she would like everyone to believe. Even with all the plastic surgery she's had done, which of course she would never admit to, she isn't as young as she once was." I suddenly felt really sad for Joan. "Come on, Dot. I feel like we're intruding by watching them. Let's go."

"Okay, I guess you're right. At least we know that there's actually something between them and it's not just Fiona's imagination. That makes me even more certain that we need to talk to Fiona. Now we have some solid proof that he's not being faithful."

As we roused the dogs to leave, we continued to watch the couple. We were surprised to see Joan shaking her head and beginning to cry. A sneer spread across Mason's face, and he slammed his fist down on the table. Joan stood, reached across the table, and slapped him. He grabbed her by the wrist, but she jerked away and rushed past without even noticing us.

"Well, that looked like a break-up if I've ever seen one," I commented. I could only imagine from the look on Joan's face, that Mason had said some horrible things that upset her. I was finding more and more reasons to dislike the guy. He really wasn't a nice person.

Mason threw some money on the table, got up and left. He pulled out of the parking lot in the direction of Palm Gardens.

"Still up for that swim?" Dot stood and nudged her chair back up to the table. Magnum stood ready at her side. "I could use it after witnessing all this drama. A good swim always de-stresses me."

"That sounds wonderful. Maybe it's early enough that there won't be a crowd at the pool, yet." I stood as Angus jumped from my lap, bouncing and ready to go.

I WAS READY AND WAITING in a chair on the front porch when Dot walked up the sidewalk. It was still a little early for many of the residents to be out and about, so it was the best time, in my opinion, to go to the pool. It's what I liked most about Palm Gardens. In a 55+ senior community like ours, there were no children allowed, except for short visits, so the pool was always a welcome relaxation.

"Don't you just love the fact that there are very rarely kids screaming and splashing at our pool?" I asked as we started on the short walk to the Rec Center. "I mean, I love spending time with my grandchildren when they come to visit, but I have to admit, the quiet of the community is the thing I love the most."

"It's definitely one of the things that drew me to Palm Gardens. It's quite a drastic change from the noisy big city. No honking horns and constant sirens. It was a bit of a culture shock at first, but I love it here. Not just our little community, but the whole town of Palm Grove is so quaint and friendly. I'm really glad I made this decision."

"Have you ever regretted not getting married or having a family?" I asked, hoping I wasn't prying too much.

"I don't think I'm really cut out to be a wife and certainly not a mother. I'm not sure I have a nurturing bone in my body," she laughed. "I know it's hard for you to believe since you had such a wonderful marriage, but I'm happy on my own. I like making my own decisions and doing what I want when I want."

Dot had entered the academy right out of college and worked her way up to retire as a detective. She was the quintessential example of the career cop and never wanted any "romantic entanglements," as she called them. She had been one hundred percent married to the job.

"The law enforcement life has to be hard on families. I totally understand," I said, and truly meant it. But I also knew that, in being a cop, she had missed out on a lot of the normal life things, like parties, vacations, and girls' nights out. At the age of sixty she was becoming acquainted with a whole new world...and I was determined to show it to her.

Debating the pros and cons of living in a place with no snow, we strolled on down the sidewalk lined with gardenias and night-blooming jasmine.

I took in a long whiff. "Ahhh, isn't that the most intoxicating scent?" I breathed it in as we reached the pool gate. The outdoor pool was much larger than the indoor where they held the classes. While the indoor pool had that muggy, clinical smell, the outdoor pool area was a tropical paradise. There were two sparkling, saltwater pools end to end, separated by a large seating area and lined on both sides with towering palms, lounge chairs and private cabanas. It was more like a resort than a community pool. Water features at both ends of the Olympic-length pools gave it a spa-like ambiance.

Dot tapped her resident code into the keypad, and we walked through the gate.

"This is perfect." I threw my towel and pool bag on one of the chaise lounges, kicked off my flip flops, and walked to the edge, dipping a toe in.

"You were right. Not a soul in sight," Dot said tossing her things onto the chair next to mine and hopping straight in. She looked up at me, still testing the water. "Come on, you big sissy. Get in."

I took a deep breath and jumped in. It was the middle of the summer in Florida, so any water felt good, but this was perfect. After a few minutes of splashing and laughter, I swam to the side and did some leg exercises while Dot moved to the designated lap lane and began her laps. I closed my eyes and relaxed to the sound of running water features, enjoying the warm sun streaming through the palm branches. Satisfied I'd done enough scissor kicks, I climbed out and toweled off.

Putting in my ear buds, I selected my favorite country music playlist, laid face down on the chaise lounge and soon dozed off.

"You're turning pink, you better turn over," Dot roused several minutes later as she settled into the other deck chair.

I sat upright and put on my sun hat to shade my face. I noticed that while I had dozed, several more residents had wandered in and were scattered along the large poolside relaxing in the chaise lounges. "Dot, what's the most exciting place you've ever visited?" I asked as I slathered on another layer of cocoa butter sunscreen.

Dot scrunched up her face in thought. "Most exciting? I guess it would be Wrigley Field."

"A baseball field? That's the most exciting place you've ever been?" I cocked an eyebrow and turned to face her. I definitely needed to get to work on that whole new world of fun list.

"Some of my friends from college took me to a Cubs game to celebrate being accepted into the Police Academy. That was in 1984 and the Cubs were killing it." Dot's eyes lit up as she talked about what was obviously a special day. "We were lucky enough to see Ryne Sandberg hit a couple of homers. They shoulda made it to the series that year." She shook her head. "Stinkin' Padres."

"That sounds fun, but I mean a real vacation," I said. "Like to the beach or to the mountains, just to get away."

"I've never been on a vacation. This move to Florida was the first time I'd ever been out of the state of Illinois." She stared off into the distance. "My parents worked seven days a week at the factory and once I got the job on the force, I focused on that. No time for tiddlywinks when you're fighting crime." She winked. "How about you? It must've been nice having Eddie to enjoy trips with."

I sighed and shook my head. "There were no trips. We didn't even go on a proper honeymoon. He was just getting the restaurant off the ground. We couldn't afford to leave it, and we didn't have anyone to keep it open. He always promised that one day we'd get away, just the two of us." I shrugged. "But it just never happened."

"We're a sad pair, aren't we? But you have to admit, Palm Gardens is almost like living on vacation, so that has to count for something, right?" Dot picked up her phone and began scrolling as we relaxed in the sun.

The sound of voices across the way drew my attention. Luther and Pete were making their rounds, stopping to flirt with every female enjoying the pool. They had stopped to visit with Fiona and from the sound of things, were in an argument about who could do the most laps without needing a breathing treatment. Fiona smiled and nodded, much too nice to tell them to move on so she could get back to her steamy romance novel.

I pulled my hat further down over my eyes and put my ear buds back in, but the solace didn't last long. Luther and Pete soon rounded the end of the pool and stopped to say hello.

6

"GOOD MORNING," PETE said, his pasty, white belly now eye-level with me. "How's life treating my two favorite ladies, today?"

Dot and I roused from our few minutes of quiet and greeted the guys.

"Hi, Pete. Hi, Luther," Dot mumbled unenthusiastically. She wrinkled her nose at the overwhelming smell of Old Spice as Pete propped his foot up on the end of her chaise and did some warmup stretches.

"We didn't mean to disturb you. We just wanted to say hello," Luther said. "Just getting ready to swim a few laps. Good for the ol' ticker, you know." He lightly jogged in place and shook out his skinny, white arms.

"Hello, fellas," I greeted. "Just listening to some music and taking in the beautiful sun."

"Whatcha listening to?" Pete asked.

"Clint Washburn." I held up my hand blocking the sun coming directly from behind Pete. "He's a young country artist from my hometown in Mississippi. His new album is wonderful."

Luther smiled and invited himself to take a seat on the end of my chaise lounge. "I love country music. It's all I listen to. Mind if I take a quick listen?"

I shrugged and disconnected my ear buds from the Bluetooth so that the music would play through the phone's speaker. "This one is my favorite so far." I turned up the volume so they could all hear.

Both men bobbed their heads in time with the music and smiled. I noticed a look of amusement on Dot's face as she tilted her head closer to listen to the song.

"That's not bad," Dot said. "I don't normally listen to country music. I'm more of a classic rock kind of girl, but I can see what you like about him. He's got a really great voice."

"I've loved country music since I was a teenager. Growing up in small town Mississippi, it was almost a given. When I met Eddie…" My voice trailed off, my mind wandering to long ago memories. "We played country music constantly in the restaurant. After we closed up in the evenings, he would take me in his arms, and we'd dance around the place like we were the only two people in the world." I blinked away the tear stinging the corner of my eye.

"What a nice memory," Dot said. "Did you have a favorite song?"

I smiled. "Oh, without a doubt, 'I Will Always Love You' by Dolly Parton. She's just the best."

"That was one of my late wife's favorites too," Luther said, beginning to get a little misty-eyed. "Nobody holds a candle to Dolly."

"Afternoon, y'all," a voice called from the gated entrance. The greeting dripped with syrupy, southern drawl. We all looked up, gawking as Joan Trulove sashayed the length of the pool. She gave a pageant wave as she walked right past Fiona and headed our way, her long legs looking even longer in high-heeled sandals.

"Lord, have mercy," Pete muttered under his breath, as a smile crept across his lips.

"Watch out, Pete," Luther admonished. "Hope you took your heart meds this morning." He laughed.

I looked over at Dot with a raised eyebrow. "Looks like she's recovered well from the drama this morning."

"I guess all that pageant training on how to plaster on a fake smile still comes in handy," Dot said.

Joan may have been a former Miss Florida—very former—but she still looked like a million bucks. Since she'd moved in a little over a year ago, we hadn't seen that much of her. According to rumors, she spent a lot of time on a book tour for her new pageant circuit tell-all and she was also on the short list for judging most of the higher echelon pageants in the south. But when Joan was in town, everyone knew it. She made it a point to be seen.

"That's my cue to leave, folks," Dot said, as she began packing her things into her pool bag. "I can only take Joan in small doses."

"I might as well join you," I said. I sat upright on the chair and slipped my coverup over my head.

"You girls leaving already?" Joan sang as she rounded the end of the pool. "What a shame. Mind if I grab your chaise? You do have the prime location for this time of day." She scooted in between the two men, nudging me out of the way with her hip as she plopped her massive pool bag down next to the chair.

"Hello, Joan. Yes, we need to be going. People to see. Places to be. You know, all that stuff." I laughed.

"Don't let me keep you. These two handsome guys will keep me company, I'm sure. Ta-ta, ladies!" She gave a little finger wave and proceeded to strip off her coverup revealing a bikini totally intended to be worn by a twenty-year old.

Dot rolled her eyes and we said goodbye to the trio and headed home. As we closed the pool gate behind us, we ran headlong into Mason.

"Hello, ladies," he greeted. "Enough sun already? It's just getting to be prime pool time."

"It's not so much the sun, but the company. You might be wise to take the long way around," Dot tilted her head toward the gate.

A confused expression immediately changed to understanding when Mason peered through the wrought iron gate and realized what she was referring to. "Yes, Joan can be a little over the top, but it really doesn't bother me. In fact, it's part of her allure with the men. She comes across as quite unattainable and most men find that a challenge. I find her quite interesting."

I cut my eyes over at Dot, then back to Mason. "You didn't look very interested this morning at breakfast."

Mason jerked his head around and looked at us with wide eyes. "You were at Keke's this morning?"

"Yes, and it looked like the conversation didn't end on the best of terms," I said. "Was Joan upset about your breakfast date with Emily?"

"Emily and I have been friends for a long time, but that's all, just friends." He shuffled from one foot to another. "I texted

Joan afterwards and she agreed to meet me tonight after I lock up the Rec Center and talk. I'm sure we'll work it out." He glanced once more through the gate. "But you may be right. Until she's cooled off, I should probably avoid any awkward situations. I think I will take another route to the gym."

"It may be none of our business, but aren't you seeing Fiona as well? Do you think it's wise to be so public about relationships with three women?" Dot asked him point blank.

He pinched his lips together and his eyes narrowed. "You're right. It's none of your business," he spat, glaring at Dot. "Let's just say I have my reasons. You ladies have a nice day." He turned and headed toward the path that led around the wall enclosing the pool area.

"I'm not sure I believe him about he and Emily just being friends," I said as we walked. "I saw the way she smiled at him. He may think they're only friends, but I've seen that look and she's got more on her mind."

"Maybe when he talks to Joan tonight, they will work it out. Fiona is much too nice to be taken in by that jerk. If he's not interested in Emily, then I would much rather him end up with Joan."

I nodded. "They do seem to deserve one another, don't they? Two peas in a pod."

We walked the length of the block, then turned onto our street and I suddenly had an idea.

"I think we should go on a real vacation," I blurted out. "What do you think?"

Dot looked over at me. "A vacation? Just the two of us?"

"Sure, just the two of us. Like Thelma and Louise," I said, beginning to get more excited.

"Weren't they running from the cops?" Dot joked. "I don't know. What would we do with the dogs?"

"Of course, we'd have to make sure that wherever we stay is pet-friendly. I couldn't possibly leave Angus behind. And besides, the boarding fee would be astronomical. There are plenty of places that are fine with pets, though."

"Oh, I would never leave Magnum behind either. He's like my child," Dot said definitively.

We walked quietly while I let her mull it around in her structured, anti-spontaneous brain for a few minutes. We reached my house and stopped on the sidewalk.

A smile began to spread across Dot's face. "Maisie, you're right. Why not? We could make a list of places we've always wanted to see and then start traveling until we've seen them all!"

I let out a squeal and clapped my hands. "I can't believe you're going to do it! I'll bet you've never done an impromptu thing in your life!" We continued up the sidewalk and stepped onto the front porch.

"You're probably right, but I've been thinking that I need to loosen up a little and try some new things now that I'm settled in."

"Have a seat for a minute," I said pointing to a wicker rocker. "Let's think out loud about this. That's what Eddie always said when he wanted to talk things out or discuss a problem. We loved bouncing ideas off each other."

The more we rocked, the faster the ideas began to spill out.

"I've always wanted to visit New Orleans," I said, excitement bubbling up in my voice.

"Maybe the east coast? What about Savannah or Charleston? I love pirate stories!" Dot suggested.

"Argh, Matey!" We giggled as I closed one eye, scrunched up my face and waved my hand toward her with my pointer finger crooked like a hook.

"Grand Canyon?" I offered. "Or what about Waco, Texas? We could visit all the places they talk about on that HGTV show!"

Dot suddenly stopped rocking. "I just had the most brilliant idea!"

7

"HOW MUCH *money* do I have?" I repeated the question Dot had just asked. "Do you mean in my wallet? Do you need to borrow some?"

"No, silly. In your bank account." She laughed.

I studied Dot's face. "I don't know, I'd have to check. Why?"

"I have a pretty good nest egg and my pension from the police department is a good one. What do you think about going in together and buying an RV?"

"Do you mean like a camper?" My brow furrowed. "I don't know. I'm not really the camping type. Too many bugs and snakes." I shivered. "Besides, I don't know much about cooking over a fire, and I hate public bathhouses."

"I don't mean roughing it, although I'm all for it if you are. I was thinking more along the lines of a luxury, motor home. Some of those babies are loaded with all the amenities of a hotel, and just think of all the places we could go! Let me show you." Dot took her phone from her bag and quickly pulled up a website for a local RV sales showroom. She handed it to me. "Here, take a look."

Still skeptical, I scrolled through the pictures showing a high-end, chef's kitchen, a spacious living area and a luxurious bath. It even had a separate bedroom with twin beds. "Wow.

This thing is really nice," I said passing the phone back to her. "Do you know how to drive something that big? I sure don't."

"I drove a furniture delivery truck on the weekends in Chicago to pay my way through college. It can't be much different, just takes some getting used to the size. I'm sure I could do it."

"I didn't see a washer and dryer. I guess you have to use a laundromat?" I lifted an eyebrow.

"Sure. RV parks these days are like luxury resorts. Beautiful swimming pools, community activities, laundry facilities, coffee shops, all kinds of things."

"What kind of money are you talking about?" I asked cautiously. "I did well when I sold the restaurant, so I have a little put back, but I don't know if this is such a good idea. When I said vacation, I meant just a little getaway once in a while, not a cross-country, road trip."

"Do me a favor and don't nix the idea just yet, okay? Let me do some more research tonight," Dot said, rising to her feet. "I'll come up with some figures comparing this to traveling by car and staying in hotels. Don't worry. Leave it all to me," she said, obviously ending the discussion. "See you later," she called as she walked on down the sidewalk.

After giving Angus an afternoon snack, I changed into some old work clothes and headed out to do some much-needed digging in the flower beds in my back yard. In Palm Gardens, the landscaping crew kept front yards in pristine condition, but back yards were up to the owners, and I had been neglecting mine lately. Angus enjoyed the sunny day, running from bush to bush. He sniffed and snorted and rolled in the grass while I pulled weeds and mulled over Dot's idea. When

I mentioned taking a vacation, an RV wasn't really what I had in mind. I was envisioning a cabin on the side of a mountain or a beachside cottage with all the amenities, not a tiny, rolling hotel room. A vacation was one thing, but traveling across the country in an RV? How would I continue my weekly blog from the road? I'd worked so hard to build up my followers, I didn't want to put it on the back burner. Still, part of me thought it might be fun. I decided to wait and see what Dot came up with.

My face glistening and ready for a break, I swiped the sweat from my forehead with the back of my arm. Standing, I stretched out my back and rubbed at the muscles I knew would be screaming at me later. I sprayed off my dirty bare feet with the water hose, dried them off and went into the house to pour myself a glass of tea. When I opened the refrigerator door, I noticed that the light didn't come on inside. I reached in and realized that it wasn't as cool as it should be. I grabbed my phone and found Stanley's number.

The call went to voicemail, but I knew he was always quick to check his messages. "Hi, Stanley. This is Maisie. My refrigerator doesn't seem to be cooling properly. Do you think you could stop by and check it out when you have a minute? Thanks."

After I poured a tall glass of iced tea, I went back out to the covered patio to rest for a bit. My mind wandered to Fiona, and I hoped again that my friend wasn't getting taken advantage of. I remembered what Dot had said about seeing older women get taken in by young con artists who steal all their money. If Fiona has as much jewelry as Dot said, there's no telling how much money she has in her bank account.

The buzz of a text pulled me out of my thoughts. Stanley was headed my way, so I walked back inside to wait for him.

"Come on in, Stanley!" I called when I heard the light knock on the front door. "I'm in the kitchen."

"Afternoon, Maisie. You say your fridge is on the fritz?" He set his tool bag on the floor and opened the refrigerator door. "Hmm...no light either, huh?" He glanced around the room. "Have you tried the disposal or the dishwasher this afternoon?"

"No, I just came home and went straight out back to do some weeding. I noticed the problem when I came in for tea."

"I'll be right back," he said and went out the side door into the garage.

Suddenly I heard the whir of the motor start up and he came back into the room.

"You just threw a breaker. Everything's fine. You should be good to go, now."

"Thanks, Stanley. Can I pour you a glass of tea before you leave? It sure is hot out there."

"Sure, Maisie. I got a minute. I'd like that."

I filled a glass and handed it to him. "Come out back and sit in the shade for a bit." I walked out the back door and Stanley followed.

Even when Angus greeted Stanley with happy barks and a wagging tail, I noticed that he was a little less than his usual talkative self. "Is everything okay, Stanley? You seem a little down."

His shoulders slumped and he let out a long breath. "I know it sounds juvenile, Maisie, but I'm just feeling a little down about Fiona seeing that jerk, Mason." He scratched Angus behind the ear. "I feel like a stupid teenager just saying it out loud, but I really do like her."

I smiled. "I didn't realize you had feelings for Fiona. She's a lovely lady and I can understand your concern about her and Mason Jacobs. Not that a May-September romance isn't possible, but I don't trust that guy."

"Neither do I. You know there are rumors that he's been seen with Joan Trulove as well." His grip on the glass of iced tea tightened to the point that his knuckles turned white, and I thought the glass might break. "I swear if he hurts her, Maisie, I'll kill him."

I decided now was probably not the best time to mention Mason and Emily. "Dot and I have been trying to come up with a nice way to talk to Fiona about it. We don't want to hurt her feelings, but we're afraid that he's just after her money."

"Well, someone needs to warn her, and I have a feeling she may take it better from you and Dot than she would from me. I haven't told her how I feel about her, but I think she's probably figured it out. The way I fumble and stutter when I'm around her probably makes it pretty obvious." He finished off the last of his tea and handed me the glass. "Thanks for the drink, Maisie. I need to get going. Sarah Morgan's grease trap's not gonna unclog itself." He picked up his tool bag and let himself out the side gate.

I sat for a while longer watching Angus enjoy chasing a grasshopper and my mind wandered. Fiona was a good friend. She certainly didn't deserve to have her heart broken and even worse, be swindled out of her life savings. It was obvious that Stanley cared a lot about her. I had never seen him get so angry. I hoped that a good talk with Fiona would help her see that she needed to take a long hard look at Mason and consider slowing down their relationship until she knew a little more about him. I would definitely try to talk to her tomorrow. I drank the last drop of tea then finished the yard work.

8

AFTER A QUICK SHOWER, I sat down at my computer to work on the cooking class schedule for the next few months. Connie had asked for the information a week ago and it kept slipping my mind. I thumbed through my recipes focusing on cool, refreshing salads or fresh sides that worked well for summer. I had also been dying to do a class on grilling fish. I knew that some people shy away from cooking fish on the grill simply because they are afraid of losing the flaky filets through the grates. I wrote down my list of recipes and smiled. These would be perfect. I decided to deliver the list to Connie in person instead of having to type it into an email. Besides, I wanted her to see how excited I was about teaching the classes and how much I appreciated her encouragement.

I slipped on my shoes and trekked to the complex office. It was late in the day, and I was disappointed to see that Connie's parking spot was empty. The main office lights were off, but I could see a dim light coming from down the hall. Hoping that Emily was still there, I tried the door. Walking into the front office, I called out toward the back but got no answer. Maybe I could leave the class schedule on Connie's desk with a note if her office wasn't locked. I turned the knob and swung open the door to find Emily shuffling through file folders at Connie's desk.

"Oh!" Emily jumped at the noise and jerked around. "You startled me!" she said laughing nervously. "I was just putting away some files and decided I would straighten up Connie's desk." She hurriedly closed the files that had been open and stacked them in a pile. "She's already gone for the day. Can I help you?"

I glanced down at the file folders, but Emily nonchalantly scooted over, blocking my line of sight to the desktop. "She had been asking me for the cooking class schedule and recipes for the next few months, so I thought I'd drop it by. I know she's been working on the quarterly newsletter that will go out next week. I'll just leave it on her desk." I took a step toward the desk.

Emily stepped up and snatched the paper from my hand. "I was just finishing up and about to leave. I'll be glad to make sure she gets it first thing in the morning. Thanks for getting the information to us."

I could tell Emily was in a hurry to leave but hoping to get an idea of her feelings for Mason, I decided on the direct approach. "Dot and I saw you and Mason at Keke's this morning! I didn't realize you two were seeing each other."

"Oh, we're old friends." She smiled sheepishly. "Just between you and me, I wouldn't mind dating Mason, but he's a player, you know. That's the worst type to fall for, isn't it?"

"I think the two of you would make a cute couple. Don't give up so easily. Maybe he just needs a little time." I winked and walked out, hoping any encouragement would push Mason away from Fiona and toward Emily.

I walked out of the complex office and looked down at my phone. It was only 6:00. Fiona's house was only one street over, so I decided to take a chance and see if she was home.

"Hello, Maisie! What brings you down this way?" Fiona called from the swing on her front porch. "Come, sit a minute." She waved me toward a rocking chair.

"I had to drop the new cooking class schedule off for Connie, so I thought I'd get a little exercise while I was out." I took a seat and began to rock.

"Oh, I do hope you're doing some fish recipes soon. I'm a pescatarian, you know, and I'd love to learn some new ways to prepare my dishes.

"I didn't realize that, Fiona. I'm so glad you told me. So, that means you only eat seafood?"

"Well, it's actually a vegetarian diet with seafood added in. I don't eat any beef, chicken or pork."

I nodded. I couldn't imagine not eating fried chicken or pulled pork barbecue, but Fiona seemed to be happy without it and I had to admit, she did look young for her age and her skin was flawless. To each, his or her own. "I was actually planning to do a class on grilling fish. Watch for Connie's newsletter in the mailboxes and mark your calendar."

Complimenting Fiona on the beautiful flowers lining her walkway, I rocked a little longer and finally got up enough nerve to broach the subject of Mason. "Fiona, can I ask you a question?"

"Sure. What is it?"

"How long have you been seeing Mason Jacobs?"

A blush flooded Fiona's cheeks and she smiled. "We've been out a few times over the last three weeks. You don't have to say it. I know all of my friends think I'm just a silly, old woman."

"No, we don't think that at all. Dot and I are just watching out for you."

"I'm not blind, Maisie. I have no illusions that he is attracted to anything except my bank account, but I don't care. What good is a million dollars if you don't have anyone to enjoy it with?"

I gulped. I'd never even seen a million dollars, much less had that much in the bank. "Your friends are just concerned. We don't want to see him take your money and then leave you alone and broke."

"Thank you. I really do appreciate your concern. I hope in time, he'll learn to love me for myself and not just my money. It's nice having someone to share things with."

"He does have a reputation as a ladies' man, and I couldn't bear to see you get your heart broken."

"Are you referring to Joan?" She barked a laugh. "That broken-down beauty queen is living in a dream world if she thinks he's interested in her at all. He has assured me that she's the one chasing him—not the other way around."

I wondered if that could possibly be the case. Maybe it *was* all Joan. Maybe the reason she was so upset at the restaurant was because he told her to leave him alone. "Fiona, I need to tell you something. Dot and I saw Mason at Keke's having breakfast with Emily Potter, Connie's assistant, this morning. After Emily left, Joan showed up and they had a conversation that didn't look like it ended well."

Fiona put her foot down and stopped swinging.

I could tell that I had upset her, but it was too late now. The cat was out of the bag. I stood to leave. "Just promise me you'll take things slowly and get to know him better before you make any big decisions. All of us are here for you. Me, Dot, Luther, Pete, Stanley…"

"Stanley?" She looked up with a smile.

"Fiona, Stanley is crazy about you. He's so worried about you. Mason has him really seeing red."

Her cheeks flushed again. "Stanley is very sweet. I promise to think things through with Mason. Thank you for stopping by."

I waved and headed home where I knew Angus would be anxiously awaiting his supper. I loved having Angus there to greet me, but I still missed Eddie. I could understand Fiona's loneliness because I felt it too.

I WARMED UP A PLATE of leftover chicken spaghetti for my supper and gave Angus his kibble and fresh water. Settling onto the sofa, I picked up the television remote and began scrolling through the channels to find something interesting to watch while I ate. A show on the Travel Channel caught my eye and I stopped to watch for a few minutes. The show was all about the RV life and how exciting it is to have the freedom to go where you want anytime you want and enjoy the outdoors all at a fraction of the cost of staying in hotels and eating out in restaurants. I had to admit it was intriguing. Dot's voice echoed in my mind. *See the country at our own pace. Mark things off our bucket list.* The buzz of an incoming phone call pulled me out of my thoughts.

"Hi, Dot. What's up?"

"Turn to the Travel Channel, there's something I want you to see."

I laughed out loud. "You won't believe it, but I'm watching it right now. I think we need to talk a little more about this idea of yours. It's beginning to sound like a great idea."

"Good! I'll be right over." She hung up the phone before I could even say goodbye. So much for a quiet, relaxing evening alone.

Five minutes later, Dot was standing in my living room with a stack of brochures about every kind of camper and RV on the market. She bent down and gave an eager Angus a scratch on the head.

"After we left the pool today, I went to the local dealership and picked up all sorts of information on the types that are available," she said handing me the stack. "I couldn't wait to bring them over for you to look. Some of these are just like having a traveling condo!"

I began flipping through the brochures as she pointed out some of the possible options available. My heart skipped a beat when we got to the price lists that the man at the dealership had given her. These things were definitely not cheap.

"What do you think?" she asked after we had looked through all the brochures. "Are you on board?"

I hadn't known Dot very long, but everything I had learned about her screamed level-headed and smart. She was a researcher and wasn't careless with her money. If she was convinced this was a good idea, then I trusted her. I took a deep breath and exhaled. "I think it's an exciting adventure. Let's do it."

Dot let out a squeal that seemed totally out of character for the no-nonsense, ex-cop. It took me by surprise, and we broke into a fit of laughter.

"Our first step is to check our finances to see how much we can spend," Dot said. "I can check my accounts online. How about you?"

"I can do that," I agreed. "Can we meet tomorrow morning and go down to see some of these in person? Since we are paying cash, maybe we'll be able to get a better deal."

"I need to get in my early swim," Dot said. "Why don't you join me? Meet me in front of the Rec Center at 8:30. By the time we finish, the banks will be open."

"Perfect. We can shower at the Rec Center, then swing by both banks to pick up the cash on the way."

"See you bright and early at the pool!" Dot beamed and walked out the door.

I sat back on the sofa and took a deep breath. This would be a big commitment, but I had a feeling that tomorrow would be the start of the adventure of a lifetime.

9

I STARTLED AWAKE AT the sound of Angus ready for his breakfast. I had been so excited after the big decision to buy the RV that I tossed and turned all night long. I finally drifted off in the early morning hours, but then slept right through my alarm. After starting a pot of coffee, I let Angus into the fenced back yard to do his morning business, then opened my laptop. Typing in the bank's website, I pulled up my savings account balance and jotted down an amount that I would tell Dot I could put toward the purchase. I didn't want to deplete all of my savings. Angus' scratching at the back door announced he was ready to come back inside. While he ate his morning kibble, I downed my first cup of coffee in no time, then changed into my swimsuit and packed a duffle bag with a change of clothes and my shower items. Knowing I would need an extra kick to keep up with Dot in the pool, I filled a travel mug with more coffee, grabbed my bags and headed to the Rec Center.

Dot was standing out front, arms crossed and tapping the toe of her running shoe on the sidewalk in irritation. "You're late! I've already been on my run around the lake and I'm ready for a swim to cool off. It's only 8:45 and the heat index is already ninety degrees."

"I'm sorry. I just couldn't get to sleep last night, and I overslept a little. Besides, I'm not really that late. You're just antsy.

The dealership doesn't even open until later." I could see that Dot was wearing her swimsuit underneath her running clothes and was already soaking wet from the humidity. "The indoor pool is so muggy this time of year, let's swim in the outdoor pool."

Dot tapped in the code, and we walked through the gate. We dropped our towels and pool bags in a chair and kicked off our shoes. I dipped a toe in to check the temperature, as Dot slipped out of her running clothes and we both eased into the water.

"Someone left their float behind," I said squinting at the far end of the Olympic-length pool. "Race you to it!" I ducked under the water and took off.

Dot joined me and caught up in no time, splashing wildly as we neared the float. It was neck and neck until Dot pulled away at the last second, grabbed the float and screamed.

I raised my face from the water and wiped my eyes. It wasn't a float. I screamed, treading water and trying to back away from the floating body of Mason Jacobs. Dot had already made it to the nearest ladder.

"Get back!" she yelled. "Don't touch him."

"Shouldn't we pull him out and try CPR?" I yelled back. My heart was racing as I paddled my way to the side of the pool.

"It's too late. He's dead." She ran the length of the pool, took her phone from her pool bag, and dialed 911.

I climbed out and sat on a deck chair staring into the pool where tinges of dark red still lingered around the body. Realizing we just swam through that water, I suddenly needed a shower. I spat and wiped my face with my shaking hands. My heart felt like it would pound out of my chest.

DEAD IN THE WATER 53

Dot returned with both towels and handed one to me. "The police are on their way. I also called Connie. She said she would notify security."

As if on cue, Connie walked through the gate, her face paling as she saw Mason's body bobbing in the deep end.

"That didn't take you long," I said. "Were you already on property?" Connie and her husband lived in a subdivision not far from Palm Gardens.

"Um, yes, I've been catching up on some paperwork in my office since about 7:00 this morning," she said, never taking her eyes off the body. "What happened?"

"We don't know. We just found him like this," I explained. "Sit down, sweetie." I scooted over and patted the end of the chaise where I was sitting.

"He's a swim instructor, for goodness' sake. How could he drown?" Connie's voice shook with panic.

"From the blood in the water, I'd say he had some help," Dot said.

"Are you saying he was murdered?" Connie's hand flew to her mouth, and she turned her head like she might be sick.

I wrapped my arm around her shoulder and hugged her tightly.

"I'm not saying anything, but it looks like he either fell and hit his head, or he was hit by someone," Dot said. "You two stay put. I want to have a quick look around before the police get here."

I nodded then turned to Connie. "Where is Emily? Is she in the office yet?"

Connie didn't answer, still staring blankly at Mason's body floating face down.

"Connie." I placed my hand on her arm. "Where's Emily?" I repeated. "We need to tell her. They were friends." Knowing Emily's feelings for Mason, it would be a hard conversation.

"She's usually here by now, but I haven't heard from her this morning," Connie said, her voice barely above a whisper.

I watched Dot walk carefully around the edges of the pool. Spotting something of interest on the pool deck, she snapped some pictures with her cell phone. "Looks like blood," she said as she followed the trail to a small, alcove between the buildings. It was out of the sunlight and looked quite shadowy, so she used the flashlight on her phone and disappeared into the alcove.

A few minutes later she reappeared. "The blood trail stops in there and this storage closet is full of tools. Any of them could have been used as a weapon." Hearing sirens nearing, she hurried back over to where Connie and I sat.

"I'd better go let them in the main gate," Connie said. "There's no one in the office to buzz them in." She hurried back to the office as several police cars and an ambulance turned off the main road.

A gathering crowd outside the pool entrance was being held at bay by our security personnel. It parted like the Red Sea and a short, barrel-chested officer emerged, followed by more officers and emergency personnel. I could see onlookers pointing toward us as the officers made their way around the pool perimeter to where Dot and I waited. Connie rejoined us and stood quietly, still staring blankly into the blue pool water.

"I'm Officer Jeff Stone with the Palm Grove Police. Which of you ladies called this in?"

"I did, officer. Donna Pinetta." Dot stuck out her hand to shake Officer Stone's and her whole demeanor morphed right in front of my eyes. She was back in her element. "We entered the pool area at approximately 8:53. I can get you an exact time by checking the gate lock. It will keep a record of all codes entered and times. The deceased's name is Mason Jacobs. He is—was—the new director for our Recreation Center."

His eyebrows rose at her official tone and a smirk crossed his face. He turned to me. "And your name, ma'am?"

"Maisie Mitchell, sir," I said shakily. "Dot and I got into the pool at the far end and saw what we thought was a pool float. It's a long way to the end and our old eyes aren't what they used to be. We decided to race to see who could get to it first, only when we got there, it—" I broke into a sob.

Connie stepped in closer and wrapped her arm around my shoulder as the EMTs pulled Mason's body out of the water and placed him face up on the pool deck. Connie and I looked away, while Dot inched her way closer so she could get a better look.

"And you, ma'am?" he asked Connie.

"My name is Connie Lee. I'm the manager here at Palm Gardens. Dot called me as soon as she'd called 911."

"Ms. Lee, this lady mentioned that the deceased was a new employee," he said, motioning toward Dot. "How long had he been working for you?"

"About three months." Connie wrung her hands and stared at the concrete.

"And when was the last time you saw the deceased alive?"

Connie thought for a minute. "Last night around 5:30. I saw him talking with my assistant, Emily Potter, in the parking lot as we were leaving for the night."

"I see. Is your assistant here? I may need to speak with her as well."

"No, sir. She didn't show up for work this morning." Connie glanced over at me with a worried look.

"I'll need contact information for Miss Potter as well as for the victim. We will need to contact next of kin. Do you know if he had family in the area?"

"I'm not sure," Connie said. "He was single, and I believe he lived alone. I never heard him mention family."

My heart sank. I'd been so consumed with the way Mason had been acting toward the women, I hadn't thought about the fact that he had family. No matter what kind of person he was, and what his motives were for his advances, there was probably a mother and father somewhere that were about to be devastated with the news. I knew that no matter what Peter did, I would always love him, and he would always be my little boy. I felt sad for Mason's mother, wherever she was.

10

OFFICER STONE MOTIONED another uniformed officer over to join us. "This is Officer Davis. She will take your statements and after that, you're free to go. If we have any other questions, we'll have your contact information. Thank you."

"Ladies, why don't we sit down over there out of the sun," Officer Davis suggested, motioning to a poolside table with an umbrella. It was still early, but the sun was beginning to bear down. The female officer took out her pad and pencil.

"Now, Mrs. Mitchell, let's get your information first. How well did you know the victim?"

"I'd seen him around, but only just met him at our first aerobics class on Monday." I rattled off my address and phone number for Officer Davis.

The officer took down basic information for all three of us, then began assisting another officer in closing off the area with crime scene tape. Officer Stone was speaking with the coroner, who had just arrived.

Dot called out to get his attention. "Officer, could I speak with you for a second?"

"Certainly, Mrs. Pinetta." He crossed the deck to where we stood.

"It's *Miss* Pinetta. I am a retired detective, thirty-five years on the Chicago Police Force, and I would be glad to offer my services, if I can be of any help with the investigation."

Officer Stone stiffened and his lips pressed into a thin line. "Let's not jump to any conclusions, Miss Pinetta. This looks like a tragic accident and until a coroner's report tells me differently, I'll be treating it as such. Thank you for your offer, but I think the Palm Grove Police can handle this without any help. Have a nice day," he said dismissively and walked away.

"Well, I guess he put me in my place," Dot said, looking at me and Connie.

"Don't you think we need to tell him about all that's been going on with Mason lately?" I asked.

Dot shook her head. "No, I hate to admit it, but he's right. Until the coroner releases cause of death, it's all just speculation. And I get the feeling that Officer Stone wouldn't be interested in our opinions, anyway."

"I need to get back to the office to finish up some paperwork." Connie got up from the table. "If Emily doesn't show up soon, I'll call to check on her and tell her about Mason."

"Are you sure you're going to be okay?" I met her eyes. "I know you had your issues with Mason, but it's still a shock."

Connie nodded. "I know it sounds terrible, but I won't miss him. It's almost a relief that I don't have to deal with him any longer. I feel guilty even saying those words out loud."

"Just the same, you have my number. Let me know if you need anything or just need someone to talk to." I put my hand on the young woman's shoulder and gave it a rub.

"I'll be fine." Connie smiled a weak smile, turned, and walked through the gate.

As she went out, Stanley tried to come in but was stopped at the gate by police. I could see him rubbernecking to get a better view between the bars of the iron fence. After confirming with police that we were cleared to leave, we grabbed our bags and headed toward the exit.

I dreaded meeting the onslaught of questions from the gawkers outside the gate. Keeping my head down as much as possible, I walked the length of the pool. I only looked up once, just long enough for something to catch my eye. Across the street, a person stood alone in the trees and hedges, looking suspiciously like they were trying not to be seen. I could have sworn it was Emily. As we approached the exit, Dot grabbed my arm and pulled me through the gate. Once we got past the crowd, I looked across the street, but the person was long gone. Stanley barreled over to us at full speed.

"What's going on in there, Maisie? The police won't tell me anything! Did someone have an accident?" His eyes darted back and forth anxiously.

"It's Mason. He's dead."

"Dead?" he yelled.

"Shhh! Come over here and we'll explain," I whispered, as I grabbed his arm and pulled him away from the crowd. I told him how we had discovered Mason's body in the pool and explained that the coroner would have to determine if it was an accident or something else.

"Something else? Like murder?" He was practically yelling again. "Well, if you ask me, it couldn't have happened to a nicer guy," he commented sarcastically. "He had it coming."

"Stanley! What a terrible thing to say! You really didn't like the guy, did you?" Dot said, stating the obvious.

"I'm sorry, but I hated the way he was playing Fiona. She deserves better tha—Fiona!" He stopped in mid-thought. "Does she know yet? I need to see about her and make sure she's okay." He took off at a full sprint leaving them on the sidewalk.

I looked at Dot and let out a long breath. "Maybe we should postpone our RV shopping. What do you think?"

"Yeah, I'm not really in the mood, and besides, my mind would be a million miles away, right now." She looked at the waterproof dive watch she wore to run and swim. "Wow. It's already 10:30. Why don't you swing by your place, grab a quick shower, then bring Angus to my house. I'll make a pitcher of iced tea and some sandwiches for lunch."

"That sounds good. I'm starved," I agreed. I wanted nothing more than to get home and wash that pool water out of my hair. Water that a dead body was floating in. It gave me the creeps just thinking about it.

AFTER GETTING ANGUS and Magnum settled, I joined Dot in the kitchen where she was piling an assortment of sandwich meats onto a couple of sub buns.

"What do you like on your sandwich? I have ham, turkey, a couple of kinds of cheese and plenty of veggies."

"It all sounds good, just surprise me." I took two glasses from the cabinet, filled them with ice and poured us each a glass of tea, then sat down at the table.

Dot slid a plate in front of me with a huge sandwich piled high with a little of everything, along with some chips and a pickle.

"I've been thinking," Dot said snagging an extra pickle from the jar before she put it away. "I think we need to jot down some of the things we know or have heard about Mason over the last few weeks."

Trying not to choke on my first bite of sandwich, I washed it down with tea. "Are you suggesting we investigate Mason's death?"

"Maybe investigate is too strong a word. Let's just say inquiring minds want to know." She pulled a notepad and pencil from a drawer and took a seat at the table.

"I don't know if we should. I'm not sure that officer would take kindly to us poking around in his case. He wasn't the friendliest guy I've ever met." I picked up a chip and crunched off a bite. "But I guess it's not his job to be friendly when a dead body's just been found. Maybe we should just leave it to the police."

"We don't have to get in their way. After all, it may turn out to be just an unfortunate, tragic accident." She took a long drink of tea and picked up the pencil. "He could have tripped and hit his head on a deck chair and then stumbled into the pool." Dot began jotting down a list of possible accidental death scenarios.

"Or maybe he hit his head on one of those huge pots with the palms in them," I suggested. "You said that storage room inside that alcove was full of tools and supplies. I suppose he could have been in there and something heavy fell and hit him on the head, causing him to stumble back across the deck and into the pool."

"It's possible. I'm sure when the coroner finishes, they will know if he drowned, or if he was dead when he went into the water. I wish there was a way we could get our hands on that information."

"What happens if they decide it wasn't an accident?" I asked. "How will we know? Will they call and tell us?"

"If Officer Stone comes back for another visit, we'll find out soon enough." Dot took a bite of her sandwich and chewed thoughtfully, tapping the pencil on the pad. "He'll be asking a lot more questions than just our name and address."

"So, if we're going to 'investigate', what's our first move?"

"Let's just suppose the coroner rules it a homicide. We need to think about who, what, when, where, and the all-important why." She flipped to a clean page and wrote across the top. Suspects. Motives. Opportunity. "Since we don't know the time of death, we need to think about when he was last seen."

"Connie said that she saw him talking to Emily last night when they closed the office and went home at about 5:30."

Dot pursed her lips and frowned. "That's going to give us much too wide a window. Until we can find a way to narrow down that timeframe, it's not going to do a lot of good."

I slapped a palm to my forehead. "There's something I haven't had a chance to tell you."

11

"WELL?" DOT LOOKED EXPECTANTLY at me. "What is it?"

"Actually, now that I think about it, there are two things that happened last night. They may or may not be important. I guess we got so carried away discussing the RV, I just forgot to mention it." I shrugged and continued. "After I finished working in the yard, I remembered that Connie had been hounding me for the cooking class schedule that she wanted to publish in the Palm Gardens News that comes out next week. So late yesterday afternoon, I got all the recipes and information together and decided to take it to her in person. It was about 5:45 and Connie's car was already gone, but there was still a light in the office. I went in hoping to leave it on her desk and found Emily in Connie's office. She said she was straightening and organizing Connie's desk, so I gave her the schedule and left. That must have been just after Connie saw Emily and Mason talking in the parking lot."

"So, Emily didn't leave after her conversation with Mason. She went back into the office after Connie left?" Dot questioned.

"Yes, I guess so." I shrugged. "Maybe she forgot something and went back in and decided to do something nice for her boss. The thing is, I thought she acted a little nervous when I walked in. Almost like she was doing something she shouldn't. Maybe I just surprised her and I'm reading too much into it. I'm sure it was just my imagination."

"What else? You said there were two things you forgot to tell me."

"I would've told you all this when we got to the pool this morning," I said defensively. "It's just that when Mason turned up dead, I got a little sidetracked. Anyway, after I left Connie's office, I decided to walk on to Fiona's house to see if I could talk to her about Mason."

"How did she take it? I mean, sticking your nose into her personal love life?" Dot smiled.

"Actually, better than I expected. She admitted that she knew Mason was only seeing her for her money and she didn't care. I think she's just really lonely. It was terribly sad."

"Did you tell her about seeing Mason with Emily and Joan at Keke's?"

I nodded. "Yes. She had some pretty harsh things to say about Joan, as you would expect, but Mason told her that Joan was the one after him, and he wasn't interested in her at all."

"Do you believe that? I mean look at her. The way Joan flaunted that body and made it obvious that she was interested in him, I find it hard to believe that any red-blooded man would've turned down that free lunch."

I frowned at Dot's blunt description, but that was just the hard-nosed detective side that I had seen many times since we'd become friends. I always had to remind myself that Dot came from a very different world than I did. "I don't know. I thought about the scene at Keke's. I can see how we might have misread that. It might have been him telling her to get lost and then she slapped him."

"True," Dot agreed. "But when you mentioned it to him outside the pool yesterday, he was pretty vague. He didn't deny a relationship with Joan. He just said he 'had his reasons.'"

"He denied a relationship with Emily, but I still think there's more there than friendship. At least, I know Emily would like for there to be. She told me that last night in Connie's office."

Dot picked up her pencil again. "Okay, so where does that leave us?"

Just then there was a knock at the door. Angus bounded out of a dead sleep and began barking his head off. Magnum barely lifted his head when Dot and I walked to the door.

"Angus! Quiet!" Dot commanded and he immediately stopped and climbed back into the dog bed with Magnum.

I stood speechless. I'd never been able to get Angus to obey like that. Dot opened the door and invited Pete and Luther inside.

"Hello, ladies," Luther said. "We just wanted to check on you after the terrible incident at the pool this morning. We heard that you two found Mason."

"Please, come into the kitchen and have a seat," Dot said, leading the way back to the kitchen table. "Can I get you a glass of tea?"

They nodded and she took two glasses down from the shelf and filled them for the men.

"Yes, I was joining Dot for her early morning swim when we discovered him." I took a drink of my tea and shivered remembering that moment when I touched his floating body.

"We were just tossing around some theories about what might have happened. Of course, at this point, we still don't know for sure if it was an accident or something else."

"We don't even know when it happened," Dot said. "The last time Connie saw him was at 5:30 yesterday. It could've happened anytime last night or even this morning."

"We saw him last night," Luther said.

Dot jerked her head up, eyes wide. "You saw him? What time? Where?"

Pete nodded. "Yep, the two of us went to grab a late-night snack at the Crazy Cactus. He and Joan were in a serious discussion in one of the back booths."

"What time was that?" Dot grabbed the pencil and began to write.

"I'd say about 10:30?" Pete looked at Luther for confirmation and Luther nodded.

"I remember Mason telling me yesterday at the pool that Joan had agreed to meet him after he closed up the Rec Center so they could talk things out," I said.

Dot added the time to her notes. "I don't know how much this is going to tell us until we find out a time of death."

"Sherry, my ex-wife's brother's daughter works as a dispatcher in the police department," Luther announced proudly. "I could give her a call and see if she can tell us anything."

"That's a good idea, Luther." Pete gave his buddy a slap on the back. "Smart thinkin'."

Luther stepped into the living room to make the call while I filled Pete in about my visit to Fiona.

"I hope she didn't take it too hard," Pete said. "She's one of the nicest people here. That Stanley's got it bad for her."

"Yes, he confessed to me yesterday that he had feelings for Fiona," I said. "He also made it clear how much he did not like Mason." I decided not to tell the others that Stanley as much as threatened to kill Mason. I was sure he didn't really mean it.

Luther walked into the kitchen and sat back down at the table. "Sherry said she hasn't heard anything yet. She's been dating the Assistant Medical Examiner, and she's gonna call me back if she can wheedle any information out of him."

"Knowing the time of death would be a huge help," Dot said. "He could have been killed late last night after the two of you saw him with Joan or early this morning when he arrived for work. That would've given the killer time to get away before we entered the pool area."

I sucked in a breath as a chill crawled up my spine. "What if the killer was still there somewhere when we arrived? Maybe they were watching while we found the body!" I shivered and rubbed my hands up and down my arms. "That gives me the creeps just thinking about it!"

"Okay, until we get a better idea of a timeframe, let's talk suspects." Dot paused. "I know there are several women we'll need to put on this list, but I think our number one suspect is Brad Lee."

I told the guys about the incident in Connie's office after aerobics and Dot told them about what she'd overheard in front of the Rec Center.

"Brad actually threatened to bash Mason's head in?" Pete shook his head. "Oh, that does sound bad."

"Connie said she came in at 7:00 to do some work this morning," I said. "What if Mason made another pass at her this morning and she called Brad? Maybe he came up here to confront Mason and put a stop to it once and for all!"

Dot wrote Brad's name on the list with jealous husband as the motive. "If he was already waiting on Mason, he would have had plenty of opportunity to follow him to the pool storage room."

"I think Joan should be next on the list." I nibbled on another bite of sandwich. "It was obvious that she was livid when she slapped him at Keke's."

"Joan slapped Mason in public?" Pete exclaimed. "How do we always miss the excitement?"

12

"YES, IT WAS QUITE THE scene," I chuckled. "She was furious, but something about her seemed different yesterday. Not confident like we've seen her before. She seemed nervous and almost desperate." I turned to Pete and Luther. "How did she seem when you saw them last night at the Crazy Cactus?"

Pete looked at Luther. "We didn't speak to them. They looked like they were deep into a serious conversation, but now that you mention it, she didn't seem to be her usual, over-the-top, flirtatious self. She actually looked sad."

Luther agreed. "Yes, I'd say she was upset. In fact, I think I saw her pull a tissue from her purse and dab at her eyes once or twice."

"Did they leave together?" Dot asked.

"No, Mason paid the bill and left her sitting there alone. She might have hung around for another five minutes, then she got up and left, too."

"She could easily have followed him. Maybe he had to stop by the Rec Center, and she saw a chance to get him alone and took it. Or maybe she went home, fumed about their argument all night, and decided to be waiting for him when he got to work this morning. It's not like she'd have to look far to find him. He was always in and around the Rec Center."

"True," Dot agreed. "If you think about it, anyone who knew him knew his schedule.

"You're right, but that means if we're looking for someone with opportunity, almost everyone could have had it," Luther added.

Dot stared at the notepad. "We're definitely not short on suspects and every single one of them has motive and opportunity." She added Joan to the list with the motive of jealousy. "What about Fiona? Do you think she could have gotten fed up with his flirting and confronted him?"

I shook my head. "No way. Fiona is one of the kindest and sweetest people I know. I just don't see her intentionally harming anyone."

"I've seen it all, you guys," Dot cautioned. "Love can make someone crazy enough to do just about anything. You saw how steamed she was at Joan in the locker room yesterday before class. And you admitted that after your little visit with her, she was really upset with Mason."

"I suppose you're right. She didn't seem too worried about him seeing Joan, but from her reaction, she was more upset about the possibility of him and Emily."

"I guess it could have been accidental," Dot conceded, taking the last bite of her sandwich. "If she confronted him about his seeing Joan and Emily and making passes at Connie, maybe they struggled, and he fell."

"If that's the case, why wouldn't she call the ambulance?" I shook my head. "Fiona doesn't seem the type to leave him floating in the water, even if she thought he was dead."

"I agree, but no matter how much we all like Fiona, I still think she has to be on the list." Dot wrote Fiona's name and again, the motive of jealousy.

Pete looked at his watch and stood up from the table. "We need to get going. I promised Lucy Bennett I'd drive her to the mall this afternoon. Come on, Luther."

Luther stood and took one last look at the list Dot was writing. "Just for the record, I don't think Fiona has it in her to kill anyone and I think Joan's all bark and no bite. My money's on the jealous husband," he said tapping a finger on Brad's name.

"I'm leaning that way too," Dot said. "Why don't you guys go out the back. Just to keep the dogs from getting all worked up. And don't forget to call as soon as you hear back from your brother's, ex-wife's, sister's whozit with a time of death," she added as the guys lifted a wave and left through the back door.

"I hate to even think about it," I said. "But maybe we should put Connie on the list. She didn't seem very upset this morning. In fact, she said she felt relieved."

"Can you blame the poor woman? She's been harassed for months now." Dot scribbled aimlessly on the paper.

"It could have been self-defense," I offered. "Maybe Connie ran into Mason out by the pool, and he forced her into that alcove. Maybe she smacked him with whatever was nearby, and he fell into the pool."

"Now *that* actually sounds like a totally plausible scenario," Dot said. "Scared of getting blamed for his death, she thought it better if someone just found him and she played innocent." Dot added Connie's name with self-defense as the motive and put down the pencil, studying the list. "How about a piece of chocolate cake?" she asked, as she stood and placed our plates in the sink. "Chocolate always helps me think."

"Sure. I'm always up for chocolate of any kind. While you do that, I'll go check on the pups. It's awfully quiet in there." I got up and tiptoed into the living room to find Magnum curled up in his dog bed. Angus had joined him, and they were both snoozing in the sunshine that beamed through the window.

"Aw..." Dot whispered, peeping around the corner. "What a couple of lazy pups."

I heard a familiar sound and hurried back into the kitchen to check my phone. "It's Connie." I slid my finger across the screen. "Hi, Connie." I listened intently as my eyes grew wider. "Don't worry, we'll be there in a jiffy." I hung up the phone. "That cake will have to wait. We need to go to Connie's office. Brad's just been arrested."

Dot double-checked on the dogs who seemed content to sleep a little longer, so we grabbed our keys and phones, locking the door behind us. I knew Dot could be there in no time flat if she went at her own speed, but she lagged back with me at a brisk walk.

"I guess that answers any questions we had about whether it was an accident," I said between huffing and puffing. "They must have ruled it a homicide."

Dot's phone rang and she took it from her pocket. "Hey, Luther...okay...thanks." She hung up after a short conversation and tucked the phone back into the pocket of her shorts.

"Well?" I asked, anxious to hear Luther's information.

"Because the temperature of the water can sometimes make it hard to determine a specific time of death, it widens their estimated range. You know it was already hotter than Hades when we got to the pool this morning, even that early."

"So, what was the range?" I asked impatiently.

"Sometime between 3:30am and 8:30am. A five-hour window."

"Ugh! That's not going to be much help, is it?" I let out a frustrated huff.

"I know it's a wide range, but it probably helps more than you think," Dot reasoned. "I mean, it's not very likely that any of our suspects would be up here in the middle of the night."

"That's true. I can't see Fiona or Joan being at the pool at that time of the morning. As for Brad, I don't think he could leave his house in the middle of the night without Connie knowing it."

"Right. I guarantee the police are assuming he was killed this morning, so that's what we're going to do too."

We approached the Complex Office and Dot stopped. "Where's Connie's car? Her parking spot is empty."

"I'm sure she's here. Where else would she have called me from?"

We walked into the office and saw the front reception area was empty. Still no Emily. We found Connie sitting at her desk, her face in her hands.

I hurried to her side. "Connie, tell us what happened. Why did they take Brad?"

"Officer Stone called about an hour ago and asked me to email him the security camera footage from all the cameras in the general vicinity of the Rec Center this morning, so I did. About thirty minutes later, I got another call asking for the video from early yesterday morning. Then, a few minutes ago

Brad called saying that he was being taken in for questioning in the murder of Mason Jacobs!" Her voice shook with fear.

I rubbed Connie's shoulder. "Calm down, honey. I'm sure they'll have this all sorted out in no time. Don't you worry."

"But that's just it, Maisie. I am worried. What am I going to do?"

Dot sat down in a chair in front of the desk. "Connie, I need to tell you something. I was out running yesterday morning, and I heard an argument between Brad and Mason. I heard Brad threaten to kill him."

Connie lifted her head, meeting Dot's gaze with a look of terror. "Have you told the police?"

Dot shook her head. "No, but I will have to if they ask. I've been in their shoes. You can't come to the correct conclusions if witnesses withhold evidence."

"Brad's got a terrible temper. He's been arrested before for getting into bar fights when we were in college. What if he did kill him?" She buried her face in her hands and sobbed. "I should never have told him about Mason. It's all my fault."

13

"DOT, IF YOU DIDN'T tell the police about the fight between Brad and Mason, who did?" I asked. "Why else would Stone have asked for the video from yesterday?"

"You're right," Dot agreed. "That's the only reason they would consider him a suspect. Who else was here yesterday morning, Connie? Who else might have overheard that fight?"

"Emily arrived a few minutes later, but I don't see how she could've heard them."

"Speaking of Emily, did she ever come to work today? Does she even know about Mason's death?"

"I gave the police her contact information, so they might have talked to her. I tried to call her several times, but it went straight to voicemail."

I suddenly remembered the person I saw standing in the trees outside the pool. "I know this sounds crazy, but I could've sworn that I saw Emily standing across the street when we were leaving the pool this morning."

Connie searched around in her desk drawer for a tissue. "If she was on the property, why wouldn't she come to work?" She sniffed and dabbed at her eyes.

"I wondered the same thing," I said leaning back onto the desk. "Maybe she was just so upset about Mason that she couldn't handle it and just had to get away and process everything. She confided in me just last night that she would like to be more than friends with him, but he wasn't interested. I can't imagine why not. Emily's such a cute little thing."

"Last night?" Connie's voice grew louder. "When did you see Emily last night? When I left at 5:30, she was standing next to her car talking with Mason. I assumed she was about to leave as well."

"I came by about 5:45 to drop off the recipes for the next few cooking classes. She was in here straightening your desk, so I gave the list to her. She said she'd make sure you got it first thing this morning."

"I did notice that my desk had been rearranged when I came in this morning." Connie shuffled through some papers on her desk before picking up the list I was referring to. "Here's the info, but I can't imagine why she came back in here after we'd locked up the office for the night." Connie's forehead wrinkled in confusion.

"Did you actually see her drive away? Maybe she forgot something and had to come back inside after you pulled out of the parking lot."

"No, she was still talking with Mason. I said goodnight to both of them and drove away. There's something strange going on. It's just odd that she didn't let me know she wasn't coming in today. It's really not like her to be a no-show."

"Connie, could you show us the same video you sent to Officer Stone?" Dot asked. "I'd like to see who else might be on it. Maybe if we know that, we can steer the police away from Brad."

"Sure, if you think it will help." She clicked a few times on her computer and several camera angles popped onto the screen. She selected the one with a clear view of the front door of the office. "This is the footage from the camera outside the main office entrance this morning."

"What time did you say you arrived for work this morning?" I asked.

"Um, I think it was around 7:00. Why? Surely you don't think I killed Mason, do you?" Connie raised her voice.

"No, honey," I reassured her. "We're just trying to get a good timeline."

"I noticed your car isn't in your usual parking spot," Dot said.

"My car is in the shop. Brad dropped me off this morning."

"You mean Brad was on the premises this morning?" Dot stood up and walked around the desk.

Connie immediately looked up, realizing that she had just placed her husband at the scene of a murder with plenty of motive." She gave a slow nod. "But he couldn't possibly have done this...could he?"

"Let's get a look at that video."

Dot and I huddled around Connie's screen to get a good look. She scrolled the video over to the 6:00 mark, and we began watching. Nothing happened for about an hour as she quickly fast forwarded through the footage. At the 7:00 mark, Brad drove up to the office lot and Connie got out.

"Okay, so Brad dropped you off, and I'm assuming he left?"

"Yes, he didn't even get out of the car." Connie's eyes widened and she took in a quick breath.

"What's wrong?" I asked, noticing a flash of panic in her eyes.

"We had been arguing all the way to work from the house. He accused me of flirting with Mason. I tried to explain that I hadn't done anything to give Mason the idea that I was remotely interested in him, but I'm not sure Brad believed me. He was livid when I got out of the car."

Dot shot me a concerned look. "It's too bad that the camera doesn't show a view of the parking lot. It would have been better if we could verify that Brad did indeed leave the complex. The police will say it would have been simple for him to park his car after he let you out and wait on Mason to arrive."

"And you can't see the gated pool entrance from this camera view. Is there another camera that gets a good view of that?" I asked.

"No. Well, there is one, but it's been out of order for a few weeks. Stanley is supposed to be taking care of it, but so far it's still down."

"Okay. Let's move on to the footage from inside the pool area," Dot said. "Maybe we can see who enters the gate from that angle."

Connie closed the screen and clicked on a different one. This one showed all of the pool, but just barely reached the entrances at both ends of the pool area. The far end was the entrance into the indoor pool area and the Rec Center. The opposite end was the wrought iron gated entrance that flanked the office area.

"Officer Stone asked for everything from 3:00 this morning. Do you want to start there?"

"You can pull that up, but I don't expect to see any activity until later," Dot said.

DEAD IN THE WATER

Connie found the time stamp they were looking for and started the video. She zoomed through several hours of nothing but a couple of cats wondering through the area. The sun came up, and she stopped at the 6:30 mark when someone walked into view.

"That's Emily!" Connie cried. "She *was* here this morning?"

We watched as Emily walked around the pool area. She appeared to be looking for someone or something. She even walked into the alcove where the pool supply closet was located, then came back out. She seemed to be calling out, but getting no response, she disappeared through the pool gate the same way she came in.

"Obviously, she didn't hang around, because she wasn't here when you arrived at 7:00, Dot said

We turned our attention back to the screen.

"There's Mason, arriving for the day," I said as we watched him enter the pool area from the direction of the indoor pool at 7:05. "That's about the time you came to work, Connie. Are you sure you didn't see him at all this morning?"

"No, I swear I didn't." she said defensively. "He usually stops by my office if he knows I'm here alone and makes some lewd remarks, but today he must've gone straight into the Rec Center."

We watched him walk around the perimeter of the pool, stopping a couple of times to pick up trash or to straighten a deck chair. Suddenly, he turned and looked toward the outside pool gate.

"Look! Isn't that Fiona?" Connie asked, as we watched the woman walk up to Mason. She was obviously distraught, gesturing with her hands in the air as she talked. He placed his hands on her shoulders and forced her to sit down at a poolside table. He took her hands in his and continued to talk for a good twenty minutes. All the while, Fiona looking more and more angry, finally pulled her hands away and quickly stood. When he tried to get her to sit back down, she reached over and slapped him across the face, turned on her heel and stomped away.

"That didn't look like it ended well," Dot observed. "Slapped by three different women in two days. I'd say he's not having a good week."

"He had no idea how much worse it was about to get," I said soberly.

14

WE WATCHED AS MASON got up from the table and continued his pool duties. He knelt beside the pool and dipped in the test strip to check the salt, pH, and other chemical levels, something Dot said she had seen him do many times during her early swims. He looked up and waved to someone. Stanley came into the camera's view from the direction of the indoor pool carrying his tool bag. He disappeared into the alcove with the closet but came right back out with a shovel and walked toward the opposite exit. You could barely see the iron gate open as he went out. The time on the screen said 7:31.

"Is that alcove a dead end or is it a breezeway that you can walk through and out the other side?" I wondered, trying to envision it in my mind.

"It's a breezeway," Connie confirmed. "The other end is right up next to this office building. There are so many hedges along that side, no one really uses that access. It's shaded from the sun, so it's really dark and creepy. I never go in there. It's full of spiders."

"Would someone be able to get to that closet without being seen by the camera?" I asked.

"I guess it's possible," Connie said. "Especially, if they were familiar with the pool area or if they were taking extra care not to be seen."

Mason disappeared and reappeared several times from the view of the camera over the next several minutes, then the gate opened, and Joan walked in. She was wearing the same floppy sun hat and the big, oversized sunglasses we'd seen at Keke's, but now she was wearing the very skimpy orange bikini she'd donned for Luther and Pete at the pool. Mason stopped what he was doing and stood, smiling, with his hands on his hips as she walked toward him. She wore heeled sandals and a sheer, flowing ankle-length cover up. Her walk from the gate to the other end of the long pool seemed to be in slow motion.

"Am I the only one that feels like I'm watching a pageant instead of security footage?" Dot asked incredulously.

Joan moved like she was on the catwalk, her long legs taking smooth strides, and Mason never took his eyes off her. She walked up to him, wrapped her arms around his neck and planted a long kiss on his lips.

"Whoa! I never saw that coming," I said. "Not after the scene at the restaurant."

"Whatever happened earlier, I guess they got it worked out," Connie said. "She's such a cougar."

We watched as they flirted for a few minutes. Joan placed her hand lovingly on his cheek, then floated off through the pool gate, giving him a little finger wave as she walked away. The time on the computer screen read 8:20.

Dot looked at me. "I was just finishing my run and about to be outside the front of the Rec Center waiting on you. We must have just missed her by minutes. She left through the other gate before we came in through the building and cut through the indoor pool area." Dot reached over and paused the video.

"It's going to happen any minute. Are you two okay with seeing this?"

"I...I've never seen anyone die before," Connie gulped.

"Connie, why don't you go home and try to get some rest. I'm sure that Brad will be home soon." I placed my hand on her shoulder. "Surely there's no way they had enough evidence to hold him. Not after all we've seen on this video."

"I think I will," Connie finally said reluctantly. "Thank you both for being such good friends. Can you lock the office when you're finished?"

Dot nodded and waited for Connie to leave. "Well, so far we've seen that every one of our suspects had opportunity and knew exactly where Mason was. Are you ready?"

I nodded and Dot restarted the video. It didn't take long for Mason to pick up a pool net and head toward the alcove.

My heart was pounding out of my chest, knowing I was about to witness an actual murder.

Our eyes were glued to the screen as Mason walked out of the camera's view. Within a few seconds we watched him stumble out of the alcove holding his head. He staggered toward a nearby table. Losing his balance, he tripped and fell facedown into the pool. He never moved again.

My hands shook and I pinched my eyes shut.

"Are you okay?" Dot asked, her usual blunt, detective tone now sympathetic.

I nodded. "It's just sad. I know he was a horrible person, but he was still a human being."

"I was so focused on watching Mason, I didn't notice the alcove," Dot said. "I'm going to run it back and see if we can catch a glimpse of anything that will tell us who is in there."

Dot used the mouse and moved the video back a few seconds, then stared intently at the screen.

"I just can't see anything." Dot frowned and let out a frustrated huff. "The killer is totally hidden. They had to be aware of what they were doing. I have to believe that this was calculated and planned. Anyone in a rage or argument with Mason wouldn't have taken the care to stay out of sight. The normal tendency would have been to go after him when he staggered away. Even just a few steps and we should have been able to see them. If it was an accident, surely they would have tried to save him." She paused. "No. This was intentional, cold-blooded murder."

I jumped at a knock on the office door. "Mrs. Lee, this is Officer Stone. I need to speak with you." I looked at Dot and she quickly logged off the security footage while I walked to the door.

Surprised, his eyebrows shot up as he glanced past me and around the small office. "Ladies, I didn't expect to see you here. I need to talk to Mrs. Lee. Where is she?"

"Connie called us, distraught over her husband being accused of murder, so we came over to try to calm her down." I frowned at Stone. "She was still pretty upset, so we sent her home to rest."

"I assured her that you didn't have enough to hold him and that I was sure he would be released soon." Dot smiled politely.

"Oh, you did? How do you know what evidence I have on him?"

"Like I said, I was a homicide detective for thirty-five years. Connie said you picked him up within thirty minutes of viewing the security footage she sent you. I knew you didn't have anything on him other than the fact that he had an argument with the deceased yesterday morning."

"How did you know that?"

"I was passing the Rec Center on my morning jog around the lake when I heard them arguing outside the building, then Brad got in his car and drove off." Dot eyed the officer. "Now, it's your turn to answer the million-dollar question. How did *you* know about the argument? As far as Connie knew, there was no one else around to witness it. Someone must have told you about it or you wouldn't have asked for yesterday's video footage."

"That's privileged information. I'm not discussing an active case with you, big city ex-detective or not." He glared right back at her. It was a battle of wills. "I know it might be hard for you to believe, but we do know how to conduct a murder investigation down here." He took a small pad and pencil from his shirt pocket. "Now, you said you heard what was said in the argument? What were Mr. Lee's exact words?"

Dot hesitated.

I knew Dot felt the same way I did. Brad was the logical suspect and could be guilty, but something in my gut told me he didn't kill Mason.

"Miss Pinetta? His exact words?"

"If I ever hear of you making another pass at my wife, I'll bash your skull in." Dot cringed as she said the words. That's exactly what someone had done.

"I see." Stone scribbled on the note pad and studied both of us. "And by the way, why are the two of you still in Mrs. Lee's office if she's gone for the day?"

"She just left. We told her we would lock up everything for her so she could get home to Brad," I said, smiling as innocently as I could.

He looked as if he wasn't sure if he should believe me or not.

"What did you need to see her about, officer?" Dot asked.

"I'm looking for a Stanley Taylor. I need to take him in for questioning. Do you know where I could find him?"

"Stanley? He wouldn't hurt a fly! There's no way he killed Mason!" I screeched.

"What makes you think Stanley had anything to do with this?" Dot asked.

Again, Stone glared at Dot. Then giving a resigned sigh, he said, "The coroner has identified the murder weapon as a large plumber's wrench. I understand that Mr. Taylor is the head of maintenance here. I just need to see his wrenches."

"That's not enough of a reason to take him in. You can do that here on the premises," Dot argued.

Stone looked away. "Just tell me where I can find him."

"There's something else, isn't there?" she said as if she recognized his tactic of avoiding eye contact.

Stone blew out an irritated breath. "After questioning some of the residents here, we believe that Mr. Taylor has feelings for a Mrs. Fiona Scranton, who I'm told the deceased was planning to marry. According to those residents, Mr. Taylor had voiced concerns that the deceased was trying to steal Mrs. Scranton's money and was determined to stop him." He stopped and stared pointedly at them. "Now. I'll ask you again. Where can I find Mr. Taylor?"

"Let me guess. Those residents wouldn't happen to be named Pete and Luther, would they?" I asked.

"Yes, I believe that is, in fact, their names. Why?"

"You have to understand, officer. Males here in Palm Gardens outnumber the females three to one, so some of the men can be a little cutthroat when it comes to the competition. Those two have had their eyes on Fiona and Joan, and they would do whatever it took, aside from murder, of course, to sideline the competition, namely Stanley."

"People have killed for less, ma'am. Ninety-nine percent of all murders come down to three simple motives. Money, love, or revenge. Whether you think he's capable of doing it or not, I'm still going to need to take him down to the station for questioning."

Dot frowned, realizing Stone wasn't leaving without Stanley. "He lives in the first home on the right after you cross Mimosa. I think the number is 4009."

"Thank you." He turned and walked out.

For the first time, I saw fear cross Dot's face.

15

DOT'S VOICE HELD A hint of panic. "Do you remember when we stopped and talked with Stanley on the way to aerobics class? He said that if Mason gave us any trouble to let him know. That he had plenty of things in his tool bag that would stop him."

"Oh, Dot. He was just joking. You know Stanley would never hurt anyone."

"And then, this morning outside the pool gate. He said Mason deserved anything he got."

Stanley's comment when he came by to repair my refrigerator popped into my head. *"If he hurts her, Maisie, I swear I'll kill him."* I shook my head as if to chase away the mere notion that Stanley had followed through with that threat. "That's nonsense. There has to be more to this than just a love triangle, or quadrangle, or whatever it is," I said. "I just don't think any of the people here would kill over that."

"I've seen it all. Don't fool yourself. People will kill for a lot less."

"I know you're right, Dot, but this has just been overwhelming for me. To think that not just someone we know, but one of our friends could do something like this? It's hard to wrap my head around. I think I need to get Angus from your house and head home. This has been a lot to deal with since we got out of bed this morning, excited to go RV shopping."

Dot smiled sympathetically. "Of course, it has. I forget that you aren't accustomed to seeing this every day. And to tell you the truth, it's been a while since I've dealt with it. I won't say I enjoy it by any means, but I have to admit I might have missed the thrill of the chase just a teensy bit over the past year."

"Well, I don't know who killed Mason, but I just don't believe it was Stanley. If we need to keep digging to clear his name, then so be it," I said with resolve.

I made sure that Connie's office door was locked, then flipped the sign on the main office door to CLOSED, locking it as we went out.

My heart was so heavy, and my mind was spinning with all that had happened. "I know I said I was ready to get home, but do you think we need to check on Fiona? Her house is only around the corner."

"I think that's a good idea," Dot agreed. "I would hate for her to be all alone dealing with this, knowing how she felt about Mason. I'm sure it's hard on her."

After the short walk, we stood on Fiona's porch, knocking lightly on her door.

I heard movement from inside and a frail, distraught Fiona cracked the door just enough to see who was there. She swung it open without a word and stepped aside for us to walk through. We only made it steps inside the door before Fiona broke down into sobs. I rushed to her side and helped her to the sofa to sit down.

"Oh, Fiona. We are so sorry about Mason." My heart ached for the poor woman.

Dot handed her a box of tissues from the hall table and took a seat on the other side of Fiona. "We just wanted to see if there was anything we could do for you. I can't imagine how you're feeling."

Fiona dabbed at her nose with the tissue. "It's so horrible. The police just left. They said it was murder. Murder!" She raised her weak voice. Fiona was pure class and always so put-together. Aside from her silvery, gray hair, she rarely looked her age. But right now, she looked all of her seventy-plus years and then some. "Who would do this to him?"

"We just spoke with the police in Connie's office as well. They were taking Stanley in for questioning."

Fiona jerked her head up. "Stanley? That's not possible," she said shaking her head adamantly. "Stanley's the nicest guy I know. Why on earth would they think he could do this to Mason?"

"It seems that someone hit Mason in the head with a plumber's wrench," Dot said.

"So? Lots of people have wrenches in their homes. Even I have a wrench! That's ridiculous!"

"Well, it probably didn't help that someone might have mentioned to the police that Stanley was, shall we say, very fond of you, and that he was concerned about Mason's motives in pursuing you."

Fiona immediately looked at me. "You told th—"

"No!" I said cutting her off. "I would never throw Stanley under the bus like that! I think Pete and Luther might have mentioned it when the police questioned them this afternoon. I really don't think they had any idea it might lead to this! They didn't even know about the plumber's wrench being the murder weapon. The only reason we know is because Officer Stone told us."

"Well...unless Luther's brother's ex-wife's whatever let that slip to the guys," Dot said. "But even so, I don't think they would ever have done it if they thought it might get Stanley in this much trouble. You know how the guys are. They feel like everything is a competition around here, especially the available women."

"Connie allowed us to take a look at the security footage from this morning around the pool area." Dot hesitated, then continued. "We know you saw Mason this morning. It didn't look like it was a friendly conversation."

Fiona's shoulders dropped and she let out a long sigh. "Yes, that's why the police were here...to ask me about that."

"What happened? What did he say to make you angry enough to slap him?" I asked.

"After you left last night, I did some serious thinking. I realized it was pathetic of me to be carrying on with a young man like Mason, especially when I knew he had no real interest in me. I decided I was going to break it off. I tried to call him late last night, but he didn't answer, and he never returned my call. I knew I needed to get it over with before I changed my mind. I wanted to tell him in person, and I figured the best thing to do was find him first thing this morning while no one else was around."

"From the looks of the video, he didn't take it well."

"No." She dabbed the tissue at the corner of her eye. "I really didn't think he would care. It's not like he was in love with me. But he had a fit. He kept saying, 'I'm not letting you do this to me. We've worked too hard for this.'"

"Worked too hard for what?" I asked.

"That's when I realized it was all a job to him. All the 'work' he put into courting me just to get to my money. He said he'd spent too much time and money on a shriveled-up, old lady and he was tired of smelling like moth balls. That's when I slapped him and left."

"What cruel things to say. I'm so sorry." I reached around Fiona's shoulders and hugged her close.

"Are you sure he said 'we've' worked too hard for this? Who is 'we?'"

Fiona thought for a minute. "Yes, I'm sure he said 'we.' I guess he meant the two of us?"

"I guess so. It just seems like an odd thing to say," Dot said.

"I hate that the last time we spoke ended so badly, and I hope they find out who did this to Mason, but you have to believe me. I didn't kill him. I was ready to be done with our relationship, but I certainly didn't want anything bad to happen to him…no matter how cruel he could be."

"Of course, you didn't," I reassured her. "We need to get going now and check on the dogs. "We just wanted you to know that we are here for you if you need anything at all. You can call us anytime."

We stood, said our goodbyes, and left.

"I feel so bad for her," I said on the walk back. "We really need to make an effort to keep her busy over the next few weeks. I didn't realize how lonely she must've been to fall for Mason's schemes."

Dot kept walking silently, deep in thought.

"Hello? Earth to Dot," I joked.

"Sorry, it's just that something she said is really bothering me. Why do you think he said 'we've' instead of 'I've?'"

"I don't know. Just a slip of the tongue? Is it important?"

"I don't know yet. We'll see."

16

ANGUS WAS HUNGRY AND so was I after I picked him up at Dot's and walked home. I gave him fresh water and some kibble, then pulled out my recipe book to find something quick and simple for supper. Rummaging around in the fridge, I found the pound of ground beef I'd picked up a few days before and decided that my grandmother's old recipe of Beef and Rice Casserole sounded like the perfect comfort food after a hard day. It was one of the easiest things to make and had always been a big hit as the Tuesday lunch special at the restaurant. I turned on some music to cook by and gathered the six ingredients. I tied on my apron, the one that read, "Southern Cookin' Makes You Good-Lookin.'" While I chopped an onion, my mind flashed back to Mason's floating body, then the security video of him stumbling into the pool holding his bleeding head. I looked at the beef on the counter and my stomach turned over. I wondered if it wasn't such a good recipe choice after all. Shaking off the sickening feeling, I took a long breath and tried to focus on Dot's list of suspects.

Brad Lee. Did he park his car after he dropped Connie off this morning and then wait on Mason to arrive for work just to kill him? Did he threaten him again and the argument turned violent? Brad had been around the pool and office area many times. Was it possible that he knew about the alcove entrance? But if he were only planning to talk to Mason and not kill him, would he have thought to avoid the cameras? No, it didn't make sense that Brad would commit pre-meditated murder. He seemed more like the 'crime of passion' kind of guy. I mentally moved Brad down on the list.

But, if it wasn't Brad, then that meant that someone else had to move into the top spot. The problem was, of the rest of the people on the list, I couldn't imagine any of them as a pre-meditated killer. Certainly not Fiona. I hadn't realized just how small and fragile Fiona was until I hugged her. She would be hard pressed to raise a heavy plumber's wrench and swing it with enough force to cause a mortal wound. Mason had to be at least three or four inches taller than Fiona, to boot.

What really scared me was Stanley. He knew that alcove and every tool in that closet. He had access to plenty of wrenches. He had essentially told us he had a bag full of weapons when we met him on the sidewalk two days ago. But Stanley? I just couldn't wrap my head around it. As bad as I hated to admit it, the evidence seemed to be pointing to him so far. But just because a wrench was used, didn't mean it was Stanley's wrench, I told myself. Surely the police would be able to find fingerprints or traces of blood if it were one of his wrenches. Maybe that was something Luther's relative, or whatever she was, could find out. I made a mental note to text Luther to see if he'd heard any other juicy tidbits of information.

I unwrapped the beef and dumped it into a skillet on the stove and began breaking it up to brown over the heat. I raked the chopped onion off the cutting board into the skillet, mixing it in with the meat, then washed my hands. Knowing it would take the meat and onions a few minutes to cook down, I picked up my phone and texted Luther.

"Any news from your connection at the police department?"

The three dots appeared as he responded. *"They said the murder weapon was a wrench! Do you think Stanley killed him?"*

"We heard that from Officer Stone. He took Stanley in for questioning earlier because someone told them about his feelings for Fiona."

I waited but got no response from Luther. I was just about to text again when my phone rang, and Luther's name scrolled across the screen.

"Hi, Luther. What's up?"

"Can you talk for a minute?"

"Sure," I said. I put him on speaker so I could stir the meat while I talked.

"I'm afraid Pete and I have really messed up. When Sherry called me earlier today and told me they ruled it a homicide, I might have let it slip that the last time I talked with him, Stanley was really mad at how Mason was treating Fiona and about how we all thought Mason was trying to cheat her out of her fortune. She must have told Officer Stone what I said."

"I knew someone had to have mentioned Stanley to them or they wouldn't have come looking for him so quickly."

"At that point we had no idea what the murder weapon was! We would never have tried to point the finger at Stanley! He's our friend!"

"I know you and Pete didn't mean to get him into this much trouble, but it looks like that might be exactly what you've done. The best thing we can do now is try to make sure the police don't convict the wrong man."

"What can we do to help? I know you and Dot are snooping around."

"Well, I don't know what Dot is doing, but I'm about to eat supper and try to get my mind off all the terrible things I've seen today. Can we talk about this more tomorrow? Maybe you can find out from Sherry if any fingerprints were found on any of Stanley's tools. I'm sure they are testing them."

"Will do. I won't bother her tonight, but I'll text her first thing in the morning." He clicked off the call.

I finished adding all the casserole ingredients to the baking dish, gave it a good stir, and placed it in the preheated oven. I set the timer, put on a pot of green beans to go along with the casserole, and sat down at the kitchen table. My eyes landed on my Bible lying nearby. My late start that morning had forced me to skip my devotion time. I ran my hand over the worn, leather cover, remembering when Eddie gave it to me on our thirtieth wedding anniversary and wondered what he would think about me and Dot snooping around in a murder investigation. I could hear him say, *"Mae, watch where you step. Cows aren't the only ones that leave a trail behind."* While I was more of a fly-by-the-seat-of-my-pants kind, Eddie always had a plan. He would've loved Dot. I opened the book to a favorite verse and began reading. Angus immediately jumped into my lap. I scratched behind his ears and finally began to relax as I read.

"The Lord is good, a stronghold in the day of trouble; He knows those who take refuge in Him." Nahum 1:7

"We are definitely in a day of trouble, Lord," I prayed out loud. "Help us all to take refuge in you and help us find who did this to Mason so that justice is served." I closed the book, putting it away just as the oven timer sounded. The bubbling edges of the dish were my favorite part, so I filled my plate and poured myself a glass of tea. No matter how much I tried to think about something else…anything else…I kept thinking about the list.

Joan? She certainly was mad at breakfast yesterday and from what Luther and Pete said, Mason left her crying at the bar last night. Was she vindictive enough to kill someone? She could have any man she wanted, so I didn't see her caring enough to possibly break a nail wielding a wrench. Plus, from the looks of the video footage, she and Mason had resolved any friction between them and seemed to be on more than good terms this morning. In the end, nothing really seemed to matter to Joan more than Joan, so murder, especially pre-meditated murder, was beneath her.

Last but not least, Emily. She was definitely enamored with Mason and seemed hurt that he didn't feel the same way. Maybe she got tired of seeing him flirt with everyone else, even her boss, and still not give her the time of day. Maybe she decided that if she couldn't have him, nobody would. It was certainly odd that she was hiding across the street during the chaos this morning and never came into the office to work. Was she looking for Mason when she appeared on the video by the pool early this morning? Was she watching when Fiona called everything off and when Joan paraded in and planted that kiss on him? Did that finally send her over the edge? She would've known if there were wrenches stored in that alcove closet.

I put away the leftover casserole, loaded my dishes into the dishwasher and turned it on. Our first order of business tomorrow would definitely be to track down Emily and Joan and see what they had to say. Exhausted, I let Angus out one last time for the evening and turned in. With Angus snuggled in tight next to me, I set my alarm, then drifted off.

17

I WOKE TO THE SOUND of my phone, but it wasn't my alarm. I fumbled around on the nightstand, knocking off a bottle of antacid and finally finding my phone. It was Dot calling.

"Hello," I managed to whisper groggily. "It's early. What's up?"

"Early?" Dot said loudly, as I held the phone away from my ear. "We have too much to do, to be sleeping in. Get up, I'm on my way over." She hung up before I could protest.

"Sleeping in?" I grumbled as I threw back the covers. "It's only 7:00." I splashed some water on my face, ran a brush through my unruly hair and threw on a robe. By the time I let Angus out for his morning business and sniff around the yard, the coffee was ready, and Dot and Magnum were standing in the kitchen. I poured two cups of the dark roast and we sat down at the table. After Angus recovered from the initial excitement of a visit from a friend, he jumped up into my lap and Magnum sat at Dot's side.

Dot blew across the top of her coffee and tentatively took a sip. "There's no one to open the Rec Center this morning, so I didn't get to do my workout," she said matter-of-factly. "I ran into Pete and Luther after my run around the lake and since we couldn't get into the gym, I did another lap around with them. And I mean a very slow lap, but it was a good cool-down."

I could only imagine the guys trying to keep up with Dot or vice versa, Dot trying to slow herself down enough to stay with them. "I'll bet that was fun," I said sarcastically.

"It wasn't bad. They're faster than you." Dot winked and shot me a smile.

"Very funny. Has Luther been able to get more information from Sherry?"

"He said that he was going to text Sherry about the murder weapon as soon as she started her shift this morning and he would let us know if she had any news. We saw Stanley getting out of his truck as we were finishing our walk, so obviously they didn't have enough to charge him. He was on his phone, so we just waved and kept walking."

"Well, that's a relief!" I blew out a breath. "Of course, his prints would be on every tool in that bag, so if they didn't have anything other than that, it probably wasn't enough to hold him."

Dot unzipped a bag around her waist and took out a small notepad and pencil.

"Where did you get the cool fanny pack?"

"This is not a fanny pack! It's a runner's belt." Dot stiffened and turned to a clean page in the notepad. "Back to business. I think we need to take a closer look at Emily. Her odd behavior has been nagging at the back of my mind."

"I agree," I said. "I couldn't stop thinking about the suspect list last night. Emily obviously had feelings for Mason that were not mutual. I can imagine that his interest in older women and even in Connie, had to have frustrated her."

"Yes, but you don't usually kill someone just because you're frustrated with them. I also think it's very suspicious that she was on the property early yesterday looking for someone, probably Mason, out by the pool, yet she never went into the office to work. Connie said it's not like her to just not show up."

"Yes, Connie said that she's practically a model employee. I mean, it's not every assistant that would stay after hours just to straighten up and organize their boss' office without being asked. So why was yesterday so different? If she was on property at 6:00, why did she leave instead of going to the office?"

"We've been assuming that she left when she didn't find Mason by the pool, but just because we didn't see her on camera, doesn't mean that she didn't find him somewhere else on the property before he came into the pool area. What if they had an argument, then knowing he was going to be working around the pool, hid in the shadows behind that alcove and waited for her chance to kill him?"

"I'm almost positive that it was her I saw across the street from the complex while the police were there. Why would she not at least be in the crowd outside the gate or concerned enough to try to find Connie to see what happened? If she were the ideal employee, you would think she would be hysterical that a dead body was discovered at the pool."

"Unless she already knew what had happened." Dot sat back in the chair and took another sip of her coffee. "How much do we actually know about Emily? How long has she been working for Connie?"

"Let me see." I tapped my finger to my chin. "I remember when she was hired because I stopped by the office on her first day to give Connie the cooking class schedule. I make them out for two months at a time. It wasn't the last one I turned in, but the one before that, so that should make it around four months ago. Why? What are you thinking?"

"I've been going back over all the conversations we've had lately with Mason. Do you remember when we were leaving the pool yesterday and we stopped to talk?"

"That's when we told him that we had seen him at Keke's, right? We suggested that he might want to walk around to avoid Joan."

"Yes, but when we mentioned seeing him with Emily, he said something I didn't notice at the time. He said, 'Emily and I have been friends for a long time.'"

"You're right. Emily made a similar statement to me the night I found her in Connie's office. She said they were old friends. I'm assuming that means they knew each other before they started working here."

"That would seem to be the case. Maybe they grew up near each other or went to the same school? Or maybe they've worked together in the past. Have you ever heard her say where she worked before she came here? What about Mason?" Dot scribbled some things on the pad of paper. "Connie should have some work history on them, don't you think?"

"Connie told me that she had hired Mason on the recommendation of a friend without checking his references." I glanced at my phone for the time. "Why don't I grab a quick shower and we can take the dogs for a walk."

"That sounds good. Maybe we can find Stanley and talk to him about the whole thing. I'd love to know what questions they asked him. Maybe that would give us an idea of which direction they are leaning with the investigation."

"We can stop by Connie's office and ask her about Mason and Emily's work history, also." I placed my coffee cup in the sink and left Dot at the table scribbling furiously in her notepad.

TAKING OUR USUAL ROUTE through the neighborhood, we kept a sharp eye out for any signs of Stanley. We passed the office and with no sign of Connie's car, kept walking. One street past, we turned and spotted Stanley's truck parked in front of Fiona's house. The two sat on the front porch sharing morning coffee.

"Good morning!" I chirped as we came up the sidewalk. "Stanley, I'm so glad to see you. I'm so sorry you had to go through all of that yesterday."

"Please, come visit a bit." Fiona waved us up to the porch. "Stanley was just telling me about the whole terrible ordeal."

Dot and I led the pups up the sidewalk. I took a seat on the front steps and Dot remained standing.

"Dot, I'm sure you know exactly what it was like to be interrogated," Stanley said. "Well, maybe from the other side of the table, that is. I was afraid that anything I said might be twisted or taken the wrong way."

"I don't know Officer Stone very well, but I'm sure he was only doing his job. I'm glad they let you go. What did they question you about?"

"They seemed to be really interested in my feelings for Fiona." A tinge of red flushed his cheeks as he glanced toward Fiona. "He asked me why I thought Mason had ulterior motives for courting Fiona and if I had any proof that he was trying to con her out of her money."

"And do you? Have any proof, that is," Dot asked.

He shook his head. "No, I just know that he'd not been honest with her and had been seeing other women behind her back. I just couldn't bear to see her hurt."

Fiona smiled and reached over, placing her hand on top of his.

"Stanley, do you know anything about Mason's work history? Connie mentioned to me that she regretted not checking his references. I think she mentioned that he had been fired from his last two jobs for the same reasons...unwanted advances toward women. Most of them older widows. She also mentioned that his last job was at a nursing home."

"Oh, that's disgusting!" Fiona cried and hung her head. "I'm just so ashamed of my actions over the last few weeks."

I gave Fiona a sympathetic look. "You have nothing to be ashamed of, Fiona. It's easy to get blinded by our loneliness sometimes."

"It happens all the time, Fiona," Dot said. "Some men just have a talent for lying and even the most careful women get taken in. We're just happy that events were stopped in their tracks. Not that I'm happy he's dead, but I'm glad that you are out of that situation."

Stanley stopped rocking and sat forward in the chair. "There is something that I wanted to tell you."

18

STANLEY LEANED TOWARD Dot and lowered his voice. "I thought about calling Officer Stone, but I certainly don't want to throw suspicion on an innocent person by gossiping. It didn't occur to me to mention it down at the station, but the more I've thought about it, the more I realized it might be important. I wanted to talk to you first so maybe you could get a little more information, then take it to Stone if you think you should."

Dot's eyebrows rose. "What's that?"

"George and Hannah Thomas, over on Catalpa Street, have been having trouble with their plumbing off and on for a few weeks now. I've been over there a couple of times but couldn't seem to find the problem. I've been trying to save them the money they'd have to pay a real plumber to fix the problem. You know, fixed income and all that."

"Okay..." Dot said impatiently.

"Last week, late one night, Hannah called in a panic and asked me to come over again. After a lot of plunging and digging, I finally found the culprit. It was pretty disintegrated, but I could tell that it was a photo that someone had crumpled up and tried to flush down the toilet."

"A photo? Why would someone flush a photo down the toilet instead of just tearing it up and throwing it in the trash?"

I asked. I looked up from the step to see a frown crease Dot's forehead. I could practically see the wheels turning in her brain.

"It wasn't so much what I found, but Hannah's reaction to it that was odd. When I called her into the bathroom to tell her I had discovered the problem, she took it from me with her fingertips and tried to unfold it."

"Hmm," Dot mumbled. "Well, obviously that tells us a couple of things. One, she's not the one that put it there to begin with and two, that only leaves one other person, and he didn't want his wife to know anything about it."

"Were you able to get a good look at it?" Fiona asked.

"When I saw her face turn white as a sheet, I looked down at the paper. It was a picture of George and another woman. It definitely wasn't Hannah because this one had blonde hair."

"Oh no! What did George say when you told him?" My hand flew to my mouth.

"He wasn't home. Hannah mentioned when I'd first gotten there that George had gone for a drink with Mason Jacobs. We chatted for a minute, and she told me they'd become friends and had met for drinks several times in the last few weeks. She even said she was glad George had found a friend to spend time with. She said he used to go out a couple of times a week, but recently, other than the occasional drink with Mason, hadn't been out of the house at all. I thought they made an odd pair of drinking buddies, but I didn't really think that much about it. She seemed pretty upset about the photo and ready for me to leave. She thanked me and I let myself out. Do you think it has anything to do with Mason's murder?"

All eyes were on Dot. This was her area of expertise, and the rest of the group was at a loss for words.

"Let me think about this, Stanley. I think you were right not to mention this to Officer Stone. It may not have anything to do with Mason's death and it might have come across as you trying to point fingers at other people just to get the spotlight off yourself. That would've made you look even more guilty."

Angus jumped down from my lap and pulled at the leash. "I think the pups are ready to get back to the walk," I said standing and brushing off the seat of my pants. "You two take care and Fiona, please call us if you need anything."

Fiona nodded. "Thank you. I'm just so grateful for friends who are looking out for me." She and Stanley exchanged a smile.

We continued on our way, Magnum walking perfectly at Dot's heel and Angus practically dislocating my arm from the socket as he ran this way and that as far ahead as his lead would allow.

"What's your take on George Thomas?" I reeled in Angus' leash a little more to keep him on the sidewalk. "I don't know them that well, but the few times I've met them, Hannah seemed like a pleasant woman."

"I don't think I've ever met either of them," Dot said. "But I can tell you what it looks like from here. It looks like George was having an affair."

"If that's the case, why would he have a photo of him and this other woman? Wouldn't he be afraid that Hannah would find it?"

"Some men are just stupid enough to keep a memento of their antics stashed away. I guess it's some kind of warped idea of danger and intrigue to go along with the affair."

"Who does he think he is, James Bond?" I asked incredulously. "I wonder what could've happened that would make him decide it's too dangerous to keep it in the house? Why choose now to decide he needed to flush it?"

"Who knows? Maybe he sensed that Hannah was becoming suspicious and thought he'd better get rid of it before she found it. There is another possibility, though," Dot said matter-of-factly as we stopped at the corner to cross the street.

"What's that?"

"He was being blackmailed."

"That makes even more sense! Someone took that picture of him and Blondie and sent it to him. But who would be devious enough to do something like that in our little community?" I knew the answer to that question before the words ever left my mouth.

"Mason Jacobs," we said in unison.

"That would explain a lot of things. Namely, George's newfound drinking pal. Maybe those meetings weren't as friendly as he led Hannah to believe." Dot stopped for a minute to let me catch my breath. "Do you have any idea which house on Catalpa Street is theirs?"

"You're not thinking of asking Hannah about it are you?" My eyes widened.

"No, I'm going to ask George," she said making the turn onto Catalpa. "Now which house is theirs?"

"I'm not sure. I do know that Hannah drives a white SUV. She's been to a couple of my cooking classes."

"That won't be quite as convenient. We'll have to walk down the access street."

The homes in the cottage section of Palm Gardens were set side by side with pristine, identical front yards. Garage access was only from the rear of the home from a street that ran behind the homes. If we needed to find Hannah's vehicle, we would have to detour down that back street. We were about to cut through to the access street when the name on the first mailbox caught my eye.

"This is it!" I said pointing to a nameplate atop the mailbox. "The Thomas Family. What luck, huh?" I smiled broadly.

Dot rolled her eyes. "Good job, Sherlock." She laughed. "This may be a little awkward with the dogs. Not everyone wants a dog in their home."

Just then, George Thomas stepped out onto his front porch and headed down the sidewalk right toward us. "Good afternoon, ladies. Out for a walk with the pooches?" He smiled and reached into his mailbox to retrieve a handful of envelopes and flyers.

"Yes, gotta make sure they get their exercise just like humans do!" Dot said. "Although, some are more well behaved than others." She laughed and nodded her head toward Angus who was rolling in the grass and getting tangled in his leash.

Realizing Dot was trying to ease into a conversation with George, I laughed. "Hey! Don't talk about my baby like that!" We all chuckled.

George's smile faded. "How are you ladies doing after what happened yesterday? I heard that you were the ones that discovered poor Mason's body at the pool."

"Yes, it was a terrible shock," I said. "I'd never seen a dead body before. At least not in person."

"I heard they arrested Stanley Taylor," he said shaking his head and making a *tsk-tsk* sound. "I would never have believed that someone as nice as Stanley could do something like that."

"Actually, they didn't arrest him. They just took him in for questioning. He's back home now." I reined in Angus a little more to keep him from winding himself around the mailbox post.

"In fact," Dot said. "We just ran into him at Fiona Scranton's house. He said that Hannah told him that you and Mason had been spending a lot of time together lately. I had no idea you two were close friends. How are you handling his death?"

The mail slipped from George's hand, and he bent to pick it up. "Oh, well, we really weren't that close. When did Stanley see Hannah?"

"He unclogged your plumbing last week," Dot said locking eyes with George. "Didn't she tell you? He said the craziest thing was stopping it up. Who would've tried to flush a photograph?"

I watched as the color drained from George's face. "George, are you okay? You look pale."

"So that's how she found..." His voice trailed off. His head dropped, avoiding eye contact. "I'm sure Stanley mentioned who was in the photograph. Nothing is a secret around this place for long. And if you know that, then you have probably already heard that Hannah moved in with our daughter."

"Oh, no, we hadn't heard that," I said. "I'm so sorry, George."

"Where did you get the photo, George?" Dot asked.

"I received it in the mail two weeks ago with an anonymous note demanding ten thousand dollars and a date and location to meet. I took the money from our savings and went to the address. It was Mason Jacobs. I asked him how he found out and he just laughed and said he had his ways. I hoped that would be the end of it, but it wasn't. He texted me two other times, demanding another three thousand each time." George shifted from one foot to the other, finally looking up. His eyes were wet with tears.

"Where were you early yesterday morning, George?" Dot locked her gaze onto his.

I cringed at Dot's gruff, no-nonsense technique and couldn't help but think that you catch more flies with honey than vinegar. But, then again, Dot knew what she was doing. She was the professional.

His eyes went wide in shock. "I didn't kill Mason if that's what you're suggesting! I hated that scum, but I'd never kill him."

"Can anyone account for your whereabouts yesterday morning around 8:30?"

"No. I was just eating breakfast here at home."

"Alone?"

"Yes, alone! What part of 'my wife left me' didn't you understand? I think you need to leave. Take your dogs and get off my property!"

19

"WELL, THAT WAS INTERESTING," Dot said, as we took the dogs on down the street. "We may have ourselves a new top suspect. If George paid Mason sixteen thousand dollars to keep Hannah from finding out and then she left him anyway, that's enough to send anyone over the edge."

"Don't you think you might have been a little harsh? Poor George was visibly upset."

"If my approach smokes out the killer, you'll be thanking me," Dot responded defensively.

"And if he's innocent, we may have just lost a friend."

We walked along in awkward silence for a while longer, circling the cul-de-sac at the end of Catalpa and then turning onto Grove Street.

"We have one last stop to make." I motioned up ahead to Joan's house. "I have been hesitant because I just haven't wanted to deal with her, but I think we need to check on Joan."

"I guess you're right," Dot agreed. "She's so abrasive and catty, I don't think she has a lot of female friends."

"She probably doesn't have anyone to check on her. I'm sure she's devastated about Mason."

"If she didn't kill him, that is," Dot added for good measure. "Listen, I know I'm hard and straightforward. I guess it just comes with the territory. I wish I was more tenderhearted and thoughtful like you, but I really do know what I'm doing. We can repair friendships later."

I wasn't so sure that I agreed with that statement, but I nodded as we stopped in front of Joan's house and headed up the sidewalk. Dot knocked on the door.

I thought I saw the window curtain move the least little bit, and a few seconds later Joan answered. She was dressed to the nines as usual, not a hair out of place. I couldn't understand why someone would get all dolled up that early just to do housework, but such is the life of a beauty queen. I glanced past Joan's shoulder into the house and caught a glimpse of a gallery wall of 16"x 20" pageant portraits and a glass case full of trophies.

"Hi, Joan," I greeted. "We were out walking the dogs and thought we might check on you. I know Mason's death must have been hard on you."

"Good morning." She leaned against the door frame as if she needed to steady herself. "Yes, I'm devastated," she said dramatically. "I would invite you in, but I don't abide pet hair on my furniture." She looked pointedly at the dogs, stepped onto the porch, and closed the door behind her. "Please have a seat on the porch."

Dot and I sat in the two chairs, Magnum and Angus by our sides. Joan took a seat in the swing.

"It was pretty chaotic yesterday morning, but I didn't see you in the crowd gathered outside the pool gate. When did you hear about Mason?" Dot asked.

"The police came by around 10:00 to ask me some questions. That was the first I knew about poor, poor Mason. It's just so tragic." She let out a long breath and hung her head.

I couldn't tell if she was truly as upset as she seemed or if she was just Joan being Joan.

"I was in love with him, you know," she continued. She pulled a tissue from her pocket and touched the corner of her eye delicately. "We've had our ups and downs lately, but I know he felt the same way."

Dot slid me a sideways glance. "Yes, I think Maisie and I witnessed one of your 'downs' at Keke's a few days ago. It looked like you and Mason had quite the argument."

She jerked her head up and looked at Dot. "That? Oh, that was nothing. Just a little tiff." She waved her hand, brushing off the statement.

"You were also seen that night at the Crazy Cactus, and we were told Mason left you there quite upset."

"Well, don't you two get around? Do you have spies following me?" she stiffened defensively.

"Can we help it if you seem to have your fair share of disagreements in public? We're just going by what we've been told. Did you talk to Mason again after you last saw him at the bar?"

"No." She covered her face with her hands. "I'll never forgive myself that our last words to each other were so harsh." Her shoulders shook with sobs.

I started to speak, but Dot gave me the side eye and a slight shake of the head. Instead, I picked up Angus and walked over to Joan, giving her shoulder a light rub. "We're really sorry for your loss, Joan. If there is anything we can do, please let us know."

Joan nodded slightly and never looked up. "Thank you for stopping by," she said, her voice muffled by the hands still covering her face.

We took the dogs and left without another word. I looked back over my shoulder to see Joan walk back into the house.

"She flat out lied to us!" I said once we'd gotten out of earshot. "We know she saw Mason yesterday morning at the pool. Why didn't you want me to mention it?"

"Joan's already questioning the fact that we're so nosy. I didn't want her to clam up and tell us to get lost," Dot explained. "We know she lied. We just don't know why. Was it because she thinks it will make her look guilty if we find out she was at the scene of the crime? Or is it because she really did kill him?"

"She doesn't know that we've seen the security footage, so maybe it was just to seem more dramatic," I said. "Joan is a master at making everything about Joan. She's even making someone else's murder all about her. She's lost the man she loved, and the tragedy of their parting words is more than she can bear." I feigned a dramatic sigh, placing the back of my hand to my forehead.

"That was probably the best performance of her life. Joan's a piece of work, that's for sure."

I TRUDGED UP THE STEPS onto my porch and blew out a long breath. I felt a droplet of sweat trickle down my back between my shoulder blades as we walked through the front door. I unclipped Angus' leash from his collar and plopped down at the kitchen table. "Ahhh, sweet air conditioning. That turned into a much longer walk than I anticipated. I may need another shower."

"It's good for you! Gets rid of all the toxins in your body from all that fried food you eat." Dot released Magnum from his leash and took a seat. "And you have to admit, it was a very productive morning!"

"Speaking of food, I'm starved. The way you dragged me out of bed at the crack of dawn, I didn't even have time for my second cup of coffee. How about I fix us a quick lunch? I promise not to fry anything." We both chuckled.

"Sure, I could eat something. What do you have in mind?"

I opened the refrigerator and searched around a bit. Selecting several items, I turned back to the counter with an armload of salad ingredients. "How does a southwest grilled chicken salad sound?"

"Great! Let me help," Dot said, rushing to take a head of lettuce that was about to escape my grasp.

"If you'll start washing the lettuce, I'll chop the tomatoes." I made quick work of dicing a large tomato, half of a red onion, and some black olives. Placing them all in small individual bowls, I opened a can of black beans and a can of sweet corn. I rinsed, drained, and poured them into similar bowls.

Dot patted the lettuce leaves dry and began to chop. "I hope you don't mind chopped salad. I really hate having to wrangle huge pieces of lettuce into my mouth."

I chose two ripe avocados and halved them, scooping the yummy insides into a bowl. I quickly peeled and chopped a Granny Smith apple and dumped it into the bowl along with the other half of the chopped red onion. I added some salt, pepper and a good squeeze of lime and added it to our impromptu Mexican buffet.

"This is my friend, Anna's guacamole recipe. I know green apple seems like an odd ingredient, but trust me, it's the best I've ever had." My mouth watered at the thought of the delectable dip. "And last, but not least, some grilled chicken. I like to grill an assortment of things all at once and keep them for other dishes throughout the week," I said as I cut it into bite sized pieces. "It's seasoned, but not too spicy. I think there's enough of a kick in this southwest ranch dressing to liven it up, though." I turned back to the refrigerator and retrieved the sour cream, salsa, and cheddar cheese, then stepped back to assess the buffet. "Can you think of anything else we need?"

"Some tea to put out this fire!" Dot said after licking a taste of the spicy dressing off her finger.

Laughing, I poured us both a glass of iced tea and we began assembling our salads.

"Chips for a little crunch!" I grabbed the bag of tortilla chips, took out a handful and crunched them in my hand, then sprinkled them all over the top of my salad. "Perfect!"

Dot did the same and we sat down at the kitchen table and dug in. Tuckered out from the long walk, the dogs had gone back into the living room and curled up on the rug in front of the window enjoying the warm sunshine.

20

"WE DID GET SOME GOOD information today," I said between bites. "But don't you think it's time we called Officer Stone and tell him what we found out about George? I mean, it sounds like blackmail might be a really good motive for murder."

Dot let out a resigned sigh. "I know you're right, but I just didn't realize how much I'd missed the excitement of an investigation until we ended up in the middle of one." She chased a stray chunk of tomato with her fork then popped it into her mouth. "I promise, we'll call Stone. I just have one more lead I think we need to track down first."

The look in Dot's eyes told me that she was relishing every minute of the investigation. I could tell that my friend had missed the thrill of the chase. I thought about what it would feel like if I never made another recipe. What if, after knowing nothing except cooking all my life, I went cold turkey and never turned on the oven again. Suddenly, I understood and decided to go easy and trust Dot's instincts.

"Okay, what's the next step?" I said, taking a big bite of the chicken and veggies.

"I want to find out more about Mason's employment history and how he and Emily are connected in the past. I think we need to give Connie a call."

We finished our salads and placed our dishes in the sink. I stored away the last of the leftover salad items while Dot refilled our tea glasses, then we moved into the living room. I sat on the sofa, pulling my feet up under me, and Dot took the club chair.

"HI, CONNIE. THIS IS Maisie. Dot and I were wondering how you're doing this morning? I have you on speaker phone."

"I'm okay now that the initial shock has worn off. After they released Brad, I felt a lot better. With all the arguing in the car on the way to work, he had forgotten to tell me that he had an early dentist appointment. Once he told the police that, and they confirmed with his dentist's office that he was there when Mason died, he was immediately let go."

"I'm so glad to hear that," Dot said. "I know it's been unbelievably stressful and on top of the investigation, you still have a complex to run. Life goes on. Is Emily back in the office today?"

"No, but I did finally hear from her. She apologized for leaving without letting me know. She said that she was just so overwhelmed when she heard about Mason, that she wasn't thinking straight. She just got in her car and started driving. She said she ended up in Ocala before she stopped and decided to check into a hotel. How are the two of you doing? I can't imagine the trauma of touching the body in the water like that."

"We're doing fine," I answered. "Truthfully, we've been more concerned about the others involved. Stanley is still a person of interest even though they've let him go for now. The only thing they had on him was that he didn't like Mason's advances toward Fiona and his fingerprints were on all the wrenches. Of course, his fingerprints were on every tool in his bag, so that really wasn't enough to hold him."

"We're not even sure if the actual murder weapon was one of his wrenches," Dot said. "If they are able to determine that it was, without a doubt, one of the tools in his bag, they may have to charge him at that time."

"Unless they have a reason to suspect someone else even more," I added.

Connie paused. "Are you two doing more investigating on your own?"

"I think you agree with us, that Stanley is no murderer," I said. "We are just trying to find a reason for the police to look in another direction, that's all."

"You're right. I do agree," she said. "There's no way Stanley could ever do that to someone. How can I help?"

I grinned at Dot. "We were hoping you'd say that."

"I won't go into all the details, but we have reason to believe that Mason was blackmailing another resident of the community," Dot said. "What we'd like to know is more about why he was let go from his previous jobs. Do you have any contacts for previous employers?"

"I have a few. The first one was listed on his application, but he didn't give a contact number. When I finally called to ask about him, they were the ones that told me he went to work at the nursing facility after he left his job there. I was really stupid for not checking his references before I hired him, but he came so highly recommended."

"By whom?" I asked.

"Emily. She said they had worked together before and he had done a great job, but when I called the workplaces, they didn't seem quite as keen on him. One place said he was too flirtatious, and the women there were complaining of his advances."

"Can you text us that information? We'd like to see if we can find out more about why he left those jobs."

"Sure, Maisie. I'll text you right now. And thank you both for checking on me. It means a lot. Let me know if there's anything else I can do to help Stanley."

I clicked off the call and within a few minutes received the information from Connie.

"I've been thinking," I said. "Do you think that George could have, in a roundabout way, blamed Stanley for Hannah finding out about his affair? If George thought that Stanley got a look at that photo when he pulled it from the toilet, do you think he would try to frame Stanley for Mason's death? What if he thought he was killing two birds with one stone? He could get rid of Mason and make Stanley pay for Hannah leaving him."

"That's a really good angle. I may turn you into a detective, yet." Dot elbowed me in the rib playfully. "Now, what's that first contact number?" Dot punched the numbers into her phone as I read them off the text. The phone began to ring, and Dot pressed the speaker button.

"Sunny Acres Assisted Living, this is Deborah speaking. How may I help you?"

"Good morning, Deborah," Dot answered in what sounded like her most professional, "get more flies with honey" voice. "This is Donna Pinetta with Palm Gardens Senior Community. We've had a tragedy here at Palm Gardens and it's come to our attention that the unfortunate victim was previously on staff with you there at Sunny Acres. We just thought there might be those there that would like to know and send their condolences."

"Oh my goodness! That's terrible. What happened?"

"Our Recreation Director, Mason Jacobs, was found deceased in the pool yesterday morning."

"Mason! Oh, well, thank you for letting us know. I'll pass this along to our staff. You are correct that he was previously employed here, but to be honest, I'm not sure there is anyone who would mourn his death."

My eyebrows shot up and Dot, in an effort to stifle a chuckle, actually snorted. Coughing to cover the snort, she apologized. "Excuse me," she said clearing her throat. "To tell you the truth he wasn't the most popular employee here either. A little too much of a ladies' man for my taste, but still a sad, sad situation."

"Yes, we got so many complaints from residents here that we had no choice but to let him go." Deborah lowered her voice to a whisper as if someone might overhear what she was about to say. "After he left, I even had a few ladies confide in me that he had somehow come into the possession of photos of them that weren't the most flattering, and he was threatening to post them online. He was actually trying to make them pay him to get the photos back! Can you imagine the nerve? I won't go as far as to say I'm glad to hear he's dead, but I'm certainly glad he isn't around here any longer."

"Oh my. That is terrible." Dot sucked in a quick breath trying to sound shocked.

"In fact," Deborah continued. "The only person here that would even give him the time of day was our receptionist, Emily. She was the sweetest thing. I never knew what she saw in him. I saw them together quite often, but she left a few weeks before he got fired."

"Well, Deborah. Thank you again for speaking with me and have a wonderful day." Dot clicked off the call then sat back into the chair and looked at me. "Interesting. Let's call the other number Connie sent you and see if we get a similar story."

I called out the numbers while Dot put them in her phone. She placed the phone on the ottoman and pressed the speaker button.

"St. Benedict's Nursing Care Facility. This is Maude," a gruff voice answered.

This one didn't sound quite as friendly and willing to talk, but Dot gave it her best shot. She rattled off the same spiel she'd given Deborah and waited for a response.

"What tragedy? Who died?" Maude asked flatly.

"Our Recreation Director, Mason Jacobs."

"Ha!" Maude barked a laugh. "I knew that guy would get what was coming to him sooner or later. Thanks for calling."

"Wait! Ma'am—"

"Yes, what is it? I've got work to do. I don't just sit around all day picking lint off my shirt."

This time it was me who had to stifle a laugh, covering my mouth with my hand.

"Could you tell me why you felt like Mason had this coming? I mean, did something happen there at the facility while he was on staff?"

"You name it, and it happened. He and that little sweet thing of his had a pretty good racket going for a while. I think she grew a conscience and quit, and he wasn't long behind. Hard to run a scam without a partner in the office."

Dot's eyes widened. "What part did the partner play in this 'racket', as you call it?"

"We were never able to prove any of it, but we think that she fed him information from the patients' files, and he used that information to squeeze money from them or their families. If he hadn't quit when he did and disappeared, he would've been fired."

"Thank you for the information. I'll let you get back to your responsibilities. Have a nice day." Dot pressed the end button and looked at me.

"Emily and Mason weren't lovers; they were business partners."

21

"EMILY WAS IN LOVE WITH Mason, but he was just in it for the money," I said. "Do you think she's the one that took the picture of George and the other woman?"

"I think it's a good possibility. When you caught her in Connie's office the other night, she wasn't being the model employee you thought. She was searching files for blackmail fodder."

"Now that you mention it, she did seem to be in a hurry for me to leave. And she kept stepping between me and Connie's desk so that I couldn't see what files were open." I shook my head in disgust. "He must have been some kind of smooth operator for Fiona and Joan not to see right through him."

"When you think about it," Dot said taking a drink of tea. "Fiona was an easy target. She was so lonely and vulnerable. I don't think he was blackmailing her, but I shudder to think of what he would've done to get his hands on millions."

"Do you think he would have actually gone through with marrying her and then just wait on her to die? She didn't have any children. He would've gotten it all."

Dot's expression sobered. "He might not have been planning to wait."

My hand flew to my chest. "No! Not even Mason would stoop that low."

"One would hope not, but I've seen it all," she said. "Now, Joan is a different story. She isn't like Fiona at all. She's so world-savvy. She truly seems to be the kind that would spot a fake a mile away."

"Do you remember when we saw her at Keke's? We commented about how anxious and nervous she looked. Maybe Joan was getting desperate. She can't deny the fact that time is marching on. Every time she looks in the mirror it screams at her, 'You're alone!'"

"Wow. That's deep. And majorly depressing. If you ask me, alone isn't too bad. I think she's just a self-absorbed, narcissist and thinks the world should revolve around her. When she doesn't get her way, she stomps her foot and pouts."

"That's possible, too." I laughed.

"When you think about it, Mason was nothing more than an opportunist. He found a niche that was obviously making him money. What I'm wondering is how committed Emily was to his operation. Maude said that the girl in the office 'grew a conscience' and quit."

"But if she wanted out of the scams, why recommend him for the job here?" Angus jumped onto the sofa, and I stroked down his back.

"Who knows? Maybe he convinced her he was going to give up the scams. If she was in love with him, she might have seen this as a chance for a new start— a way to win him over. Then, she got sucked right back into the racket and didn't know how to get out."

"Are you saying you really think Emily might have killed him?" My eyebrows knotted together. "Oh, I really hope not."

"It makes sense if she loved him too much to see him act the way he did with the other women. The whole 'if I can't have him, no one will' scenario. It happens. I've seen it a—"

"I know, I know. You've seen it all." I rolled my eyes playfully and we both laughed.

"Maybe she was fed up with the whole thing and threatened to turn him in. He could've been blackmailing his own partner with a threat that she would go down with him if she went to the police. She saw no other way out but to get rid of him."

"Do you believe the story she told Connie? Or do you think she's on the run?"

"It sounds a little too convenient to me. I'm not saying that she couldn't have had that reaction to his death, but I find it hard to believe that she just took off. For all we know, she may not even be in Ocala. She could be as far as Texas by now."

"What a tangled web we weave, when first we practice to deceive. That's what my grandma always said." My phone rang and I saw Luther's name pop onto the screen.

"Hey, Luther. Hang on, I'll put you on speaker so Dot can hear." I pressed the button. "Okay, go ahead. Any news?"

"I finally talked to Sherry. It's not good news. There weren't any fingerprints except Stanley's on any of the tools in the bag and they did find traces of blood and hair on one of his wrenches. She said they had just brought Stanley back in."

"Oh, that's not good," Dot said. "If they are anything like other small town police departments I've encountered, they will stop looking at other suspects and focus all their efforts on getting the evidence that will build their case against Stanley."

"Thanks, Luther. Let us know if you hear anything else." I hung up and turned to Dot. "What can we do? We have to do something. We know Stanley is innocent."

"I guess it's time to call Stone and tell him about George." Dot pulled the business card out of her running belt and dialed the number.

"I need to speak with Officer Jeff Stone, please."

"I'm sorry, he's in the interrogation room. Could I take a message?"

"Could you please tell him this is very important. This is Donna Pinetta and it's in reference to the Jacobs murder."

"Just a moment. Let me see if he can talk with you."

After a few minutes of silence, Stone picked up. "Miss Pinetta, what could be so important that you would pull me away from interrogating a murder suspect?"

"If it's Stanley, you have the wrong man."

"You've already made your opinion known about Mr. Taylor's innocence. We have new evidence that suggests otherwise. Now, if there's nothing else—"

"But there is," she said cutting him off. "We think that Stanley stumbled onto some information and the killer may have intentionally tried to frame him for Mason's murder."

"And just who do you think this killer is?"

"George Thomas."

"Thomas? I don't think I've heard that name. Is he a homeowner there in Palm Gardens?"

"Yes. You see his plumbing had been messed up for a few weeks and Stanley had been over numerous times. The last time he went over, George wasn't there. He was out having a drink with Mason Jacobs," Dot said, emphasizing Mason's name.

"And of course, Mr. Thomas felt compelled to kill Jacobs after having a friendly drink," Stone said, his tone dripping with sarcasm.

"It wasn't a friendly drink. It was a payoff. Mason was blackmailing George."

"Blackmailing? Over his plumbing problems?"

Dot rolled her eyes. "No. While George was out with Mason, Stanley answered an emergency call from George's wife, Hannah. Stanley made a late house call and unclogged his toilet. It was clogged with a crumpled photograph of George and another woman. Evidently, George had tried to get rid of the evidence sent to him by Mason Jacobs. Hannah confronted George when he returned home and ended up leaving him."

"How do you know Jacobs sent Thomas the photo?"

"George told me and Maisie this morning while we were out for a walk. He blames Stanley for Hannah finding out and leaving him. Mason swindled him out of sixteen thousand dollars. We think he killed Mason with Stanley's wrench in order to frame Stanley. Kill two birds with one stone."

"There's only one hole in that theory. If Stanley Taylor did not kill Mason Jacobs, and I'm still convinced that he did, why are there no other prints on the wrench? If this murder was committed by someone in the heat of the moment, their prints would have been on the wrench. It wasn't wiped clean. It would have been a weapon of convenience and unless they happened to be wearing gloves in the middle of the summer in Florida, their prints would have been on the wrench. So that leads me to believe that Stanley Taylor was the only person to touch that wrench. But—"

"Will you please just question George before you charge Stanley?"

"But—I was about to say, I will pause the interrogation of Mr. Taylor until I have a chance to speak with Mr. Thomas. Will that make you happy, Miss Pinetta?"

"Yes, sir. Thank you. Goodbye, sir." Dot clicked off the call.

"Do you think he will do what he said? Will he talk to George before he officially arrests Stanley for Mason's murder?"

"I hope so. He thinks he has an open-and-shut case. I'm afraid he's not worried about our theories." Dot stood up, stretched out her back, and began pacing around the room. Magnum raised his head and watched her pace, his head moving side to side along with her strides. "I'm going to let the dogs into the back yard and sit on the patio for a break."

I nudged Angus off my legs, went to the kitchen to refill our tea glasses, and joined her on the patio. Deep in thought, we sipped our tea while the dogs raced around the fenced yard. I leaned my head back and closed my eyes, soaking in the sun's rays as if they would magically tell me what needed to be done to save Stanley from going to prison. Dot's phone ringing jarred us back to the present.

"Hello...yes, sir...I see...thank you for letting me know. I appreciate it." She clicked off the call and sat back in the chair. "That was Officer Stone. George Thomas has an alibi."

My jaw dropped. "What? He very emphatically told us he was home alone. Did he magically remember that he had company for breakfast?"

"Not exactly, but just as good as. He was on the phone with Hannah, trying to convince her to come back home. She vouched for him."

"That kinda blows a hole in our blackmail theory, huh?" My shoulders sagged.

Dot jolted upright. "Not necessarily!

22

"WHY DIDN'T I THINK of this before?" Dot said, words spilling out of her mouth at lightning speed. "If Mason was blackmailing George, he could've been doing the same to other people, right? Just because George didn't kill Mason, doesn't mean there aren't others out there that hated him just as much. There may be a whole list of suspects that we don't even know about yet!"

"You're right!" I said, beginning to feel a tingle of encouragement. "But how do we find out who the others are? Emily is the only one that would know, and I don't have her number."

"I'm sure we could get it from Connie, but I doubt if Emily would admit anything to us. She's not going to incriminate herself unless she's forced to." Dot snapped her fingers. "Didn't Connie tell you that she caught Mason going through files in her office? I wonder if she would remember whose file it was."

"I'll call her." I scrolled through my phone to find the number.

"Hi, Connie. This is Maisie. When you caught Mason going through your office files, was there a specific one he was focused on?"

"I didn't see them all, but I'm pretty sure one of them was Joan Trulove's file. Why?"

"We think Mason may have been blackmailing Joan."

"Blackmailing? What could be in that file that was worth blackmailing her about?" Connie asked. "The only thing in the file folder is the paperwork from when she purchased her house here and the basic data sheet we keep on all residents. Obviously, I was concerned that he might be stealing her identity, since it had date of birth and social security information."

"It may be a long shot, but it can't hurt to look. If there's something in there, maybe we can find it," Dot said. "Connie, could you take a picture of everything in Joan's file and text it to us?"

"Of course, if you think it will help. I'm sending it now." Connie hung up the phone and the text came through a few seconds later.

I clicked on the picture in the text. "This is way too small to read on a phone. I'll email it to myself, and we'll open it on my laptop." I hurried to my bedroom and grabbed the laptop off my desk while Dot wrangled the dogs back inside. Placing the computer on the kitchen table, I opened the file containing pictures of several documents. I immediately sent them to my printer then went back to the bedroom to retrieve them and we spread them out on the table in front of us.

"What are we looking for?" I asked, staring blankly at the papers.

"Anything Joan wouldn't want other people to know," Dot said picking up the first document. It was the same one all of us signed when purchasing our home in Palm Gardens. There was nothing on it except her signature acknowledging the fact that she was aware of the requirements to own a home there. The second and third pages were copies of her loan documents from the bank. The last was a sheet of personal information that Connie kept on all the homeowners in the complex. Since all the homeowners were seniors, everyone was over fifty-five, and many on up into their eighties, the information was kept in case of emergency. It listed any family members and emergency contacts and their phone numbers, as well as all their vital health information, allergies, medications and of course birthdates and social security numbers.

"I don't see anything here that's earth-shattering, do you?" I said dejectedly.

Dot shook her head. "Unfortunately, neither do I, but there has to be something here or he wouldn't have been so interested in her file. What is the most precious thing in Joan's life?" Dot asked. "What would she do anything to protect?"

"That's easy. Her title as Miss Florida."

"What could he possibly know about her that might put that in jeopardy?" Dot continued scanning through the papers. "Could she have cheated in some way?"

I grabbed the laptop and typed in "Miss Florida pageant requirements" and began reading them aloud. "According to the official website, participants can never have been married, never had children and must be between the ages of 17 and 25." I sucked in a breath. "What if Mason discovered that Joan secretly had a baby and gave it up for adoption or something?"

"Even if that was the case, I'm not sure he'd be able to get that information from this file. I don't think it would be listed as next of kin or an emergency contact." Dot scanned the document. "No. Joan's emergency contact is her brother, Greg who lives in Sedona, Arizona."

Suddenly Dot shuffled the papers, scrambling until she found the one from the bank.

"According to this paperwork, Joan bought her house here in Palm Gardens almost exactly one year ago. What year did she win the pageant?"

"1991."

"That's it!" Dot exclaimed, sliding the paper over and pointing to Joan's date of birth. "One of the qualifications for purchasing a home in here is that you have to be at least fifty-five years old, right? According to this paperwork, Joan was born in 1965. That makes her fifty-six.

"Okaaaay..." I drew out the word, not sure where Dot was going with this. "That means she would have been fifty-five a year ago when she bought the house," I said, quickly trying to do the math in my head, which wasn't one of my better life skills. "That's within the guidelines."

"Don't you see? Either she lied to get into this community, or she lied to compete in the pageant back in 1991. Now which do you think she would be more likely to not want anyone to know about?"

It was like a lightbulb went on over my head as I realized what Dot meant. "In order to be able to live here, she had to give her real birthdate of 1965. But if that's correct, that means that she was twenty-six when she won the pageant." I drew in a quick breath. "She was too old to compete!"

"Exactly. Somehow, Mason must have discovered her secret and was blackmailing her."

"But, on the security video, it looked like they were a couple. Not like a blackmailer and his victim," I said, still confused.

"If you think about it, it really explains everything. Her anxious demeanor when she was with him at the restaurant.

You even said she looked almost desperate. Luther and Pete said she didn't look like her usual self-confident self at the bar."

"It doesn't explain that kiss she planted on him by the pool. You don't walk up to your blackmailer and do that," I reminded her. "And then turn around and kill him ten minutes later? I just don't see it."

"There's only one way to find out." Dot picked up her phone, snapped a picture of the birthdate listed on Joan's paperwork, and tucked the phone into her runner's belt. "Let's go ask her."

"Ask her?" I bellowed. "You want to walk right up to a possible killer's door and announce that you know she's a murderer? We already tried that once today with George and it didn't go over so well. I vote we call Officer Stone and let him handle it."

"Do you really think he will give us the time of day after we tried to convince him that George was the killer? You can call him on the way if you want to. Let's go."

"What about the dogs?"

"They'll be fine. Magnum will keep Angus in line. It's not even their dinnertime, yet."

I locked the door, and we walked the two blocks to Joan's house. On the way, I located the number for the Palm Grove Police Department and called.

"Officer Jeff Stone, please. It's an emergency."

"Officer Stone is in the interrogation room. I can try to get a message to him."

"Tell him this is Maisie Mitchell and Donna Pinetta. We know who killed Mason Jacobs. Tell him to come to Joan

Trulove's home at 7474 Grove Street as soon as possible." I disconnected the call just as Dot pressed the doorbell.

"Hello, Joan," Dot said as the door swung open.

"Dot and Maisie." She glanced toward our feet. "No dogs this time? Please come in. To what do I owe the honor twice in one day?" She stepped back to let us walk through. "Please, sit down. Would you like a glass of something cold?"

"No thanks, Joan," I said. "We just wanted to come by and check on you. You seemed terribly upset when we left you this morning."

"When we heard that the police are saying that Mason was killed by someone he was blackmailing," Dot lied. "We were just in shock."

"Blackmailing? How did they—I mean, where did they get that idea?" Joan noticeably tensed.

"Luther has a relative in the police department and she told him that Mason has been blackmailing George Thomas," I fibbed.

"Is that so? George Thomas? That name doesn't ring a bell." She shrugged. "I don't believe I've met him, but it's certainly a relief to know this is all over with. I'm glad poor Mason's killer is behind bars."

"Oh, George didn't kill him. He had an airtight alibi for the time of death," Dot said. "Speaking of time of death, where were you yesterday morning around 8:30?"

"Me?" Her voice went up a couple of octaves. She cleared her throat and calmed before she continued. "I'm sure I was still in bed, sound asleep. Surely, you don't think I had anything to do with Mason's death. He was the love of my life."

"The love of your life, huh? What about the two arguments you had the day before? We saw you slap him at Keke's and then Luther and Pete saw him walk out on you at the bar."

"Oh, that," she shifted on the sofa. "I thought I already explained that those were just small disagreements. We worked it out later."

Dot narrowed her eyes. "Worked it out how? By whacking him in the head?"

Clearly struggling to keep her emotions under control, Joan's face turned redder by the second. "Do you really think I would hit Mason in the head with a wrench?"

Dot smiled smugly. "No one said he was hit with a wrench."

23

DOT LOCKED EYES WITH Joan, watching her every twitch and movement. "Here's what I think. Somehow, Mason discovered a dark and devastating secret about your past, didn't he? He stumbled upon your real birthdate."

Joan clenched her fists until her knuckles turned white as Dot continued.

"He did a little math and realized that if you were old enough to buy property here in Palm Gardens, then something wasn't adding up. You faked your birth certificate in 1991 in order to get into the pageant. You were actually twenty-six, which would have disqualified you from entering."

Joan stood and walked over to the credenza against the wall. She opened the drawer and took out a package of cigarettes, nervously tapped one out and lit it. She took a long inhale and dramatically, blew it out.

"Alright. It's true. I hated Mason Jacobs and his wicked little mind. Why couldn't he just mind his own business? I mean, what's it to him if I fudged a little? It's ancient history." She animatedly waved off the statement, the cigarette perched between her long fingers.

"He was blackmailing you, wasn't he?" Dot was trying to sound sympathetic, but it came out sounding like an interrogation. Admittedly, sympathy had never been her strong suit.

"He just didn't understand. To him, it was all about the money. He couldn't see that it was going to cost me everything. I'd be stripped of my crown and disgraced!" She took another puff and blew it out. "My livelihood depends on my crown. My book sales. My career as a respected pageant judge." Her voice grew louder. "Don't you see?" She waved her arm around the room pointing to each wall covered in portraits, trophies, crowns, and sashes. It was a sad, pathetic, and quite disturbing shrine to her pageant days. "I'm nothing without it." She turned back to the open drawer and took out a pistol.

"Joan!" I yelled, fear rising in my throat. "What are you doing?"

Dot's training must have kicked in and she immediately stood. "Joan, there's no need to do this. It will only make things worse." She spoke calmly and never broke eye contact with Joan.

Joan glared back at her, a crazed look in her eyes. "One day at the pool, I accidentally left my wallet behind. He found it and brought it to me. He noticed my birthdate on my driver's license and made some comment about how young I looked for my age, but I knew it wasn't a compliment. I saw it in his eyes."

"We saw the two of you by the pool this morning on the security video," I said, hoping to keep her talking long enough for the police to arrive. "It didn't look like you hated him. In fact, you looked pretty chummy when you planted that kiss on him."

Her penciled-in eyebrows shot up. "Oh, you saw that, did you?" The corner of her mouth lifted, and she sounded almost amused. "All my pleading hadn't phased him, so I thought I'd change tactics. After I kissed him, I told him to meet me in the alcove and I'd give him a surprise. I walked around through the other entrance and waited for him."

"Weren't you afraid the whole thing would be caught on the security cameras?"

"Honey, Mason assured me months ago that the alcove was out of the camera's view. We'd met there many times for a little fun...if you know what I mean."

I knew Mason was a jerk and I knew Joan was a flirt, but I was having a hard time comprehending what I was hearing. "What if he hadn't followed you? How could you be sure he would take you up on the offer?"

"If there was one thing Mason Jacobs loved as much as money, it was sex. Unfortunately, money won out and he refused to listen to reason. He actually *laughed* at me." Her voice began to shake with fury. "He turned to walk away, and I knew I had to stop him. Stanley had left his tool bag in the closet, so I grabbed the closest thing I could find. After I hit him and saw him go into the pool, I threw it back into Stanley's bag and ran. I didn't know he was dead until I heard sirens a half hour later." She kept the gun trained on Dot and me, her hand trembling.

Dot took a step toward Joan and began trying to reason with her. "If you turn yourself in, a good lawyer can plead your case down to manslaughter. You didn't intend to kill him when you lured him into the alcove. It wasn't premeditated. You didn't bring the wrench with you."

Joan stood there, cigarette in one hand and the gun in the other. She seemed to be considering Dot's words carefully when Dot took another step toward her.

"No! Stop!" she screamed, shaking her head adamantly. "No one can find out. That's why you both have to die, too.

Now that Mason is dead, you are the only ones who know. As long as you're not around to blab, my secret is still safe."

Dot looked at me, still glued to the sofa as terror rippled through my body. I watched helplessly as Dot inched her way just a little closer to Joan.

"I mean it, Dot! Not another step!" She looked away for a split second to stub out her cigarette and Dot leapt into action.

She was just close enough to connect a spinning kick move with Joan's hand and the gun went sailing across the room. The two women struggled, sending a vase crashing to the floor.

"Maisie! Grab the gun!" Dot yelled.

Startled out of my frozen state, I dove for the gun. Grabbing it, I scrambled to my feet. Dot quickly got the best of Joan, pinning her to the floor just as Officer Stone burst through the door with his gun drawn.

I quickly dropped the gun on the sofa and raised my hands into the air.

"You can put your hands down, Mrs. Mitchell. I see Miss Pinetta has everything under control." He almost smiled as he holstered his own gun.

Another officer picked Joan up off the floor, securing her with handcuffs and started toward the door.

"Wait." Dot stopped them. "I'm curious about one thing. Joan, if you didn't go to the pool intending to kill Mason, how are your prints not on the wrench?"

Joan rolled her eyes. "You don't think I'd get *grease* on my hands do you? I picked up a towel lying on the floor. *Puhleese*...I'd just gotten my nails done!" The officer escorted her out the door and into a patrol car. Officer Stone listened as Dot recounted the events that led us to realize Joan was the killer. I told him everything Joan confessed to us and made sure to include Dot's karate moves that took Joan down.

"It pains me to say it, ladies, but...well done. I guess sometimes it takes a woman to think like another woman. Lying about my age would never have entered my mind as a motive for murder." Stone gave them a nod of gratitude and a smile as he walked out.

WE'D BEEN GONE MUCH longer than we intended when we left Angus and Magnum snoozing contentedly at the house. Dot didn't seem the least bit worried, but I wasn't so confident. We walked through the front door to find an empty dog bed in the corner. Hearing suspicious noises from the other room, we made a beeline for the kitchen to find the trash can on its side and all manner of food scraps and trash covering the floor. Angus bounced on his hind legs begging for attention, while Magnum sat in the middle of the floor, a banana peel dangling from his mouth, looking like the cat who caught the canary.

"Magnum! Drop that!" Dot commanded. The dog opened his mouth and the peel fell to the floor. Dot looked at Angus who stood happily wagging his tail.

"I'm so sorry," I apologized, picking Angus up into my arms. "But how can you be mad at those eyes?" I cooed, talking baby talk to Angus. "They had their own little adventure while we had ours!"

Dot rolled her eyes and laughed. "I guess everyone deserves the occasional adventure."

24

I TURNED INTO THE ENTRANCE to the RV sales lot and the sight of so many choices immediately took my breath away. "Wow. There must be hundreds of choices here. How will we ever decide?" I asked as I swung into an empty space near the front of the dealership.

Before we could get out of the car, a salesman stood at the ready on the sidewalk. "Good morning, ladies!" he greeted. "What can I help you with today?"

Knowing that Dot was more knowledgeable about the technical details of what was under the hood of one of these, we had agreed that she should be the one that would discuss the automotive options. I would weigh in on the interior amenities. Dot explained to the salesman what we had in mind and our target budget, making sure to mention that we were prepared to pay cash.

"I have several models that I'd like to show you," he said. "Follow me and we'll get started. You are going to love them."

Following him to a large tan and black RV, we gasped as he opened the door and we stepped inside.

"Oh my word," I said. "This is luxurious."

"Look at this cockpit," Dot exclaimed, climbing into the driver's seat. "I could get used to all this comfort. Are you sure

I don't have to have a special license to drive something like this?"

The salesman shook his head. "Nope. As long as the vehicle is under 26,000 pounds, and most are, then you can drive with just a regular license."

After checking out all the amenities inside and under the hood for Dot, we moved on to the next one. It was a bit smaller, but still had everything we needed. This one had a pop-out on the side that extended the room inside and it also had a nice canopy that could be raised to provide a shaded area while parked.

"It's very important that I have access to wi-fi while traveling for my food blog and of course, I need a kitchen with the necessities to prepare the meals for the blog," I explained.

"We also have two dogs that will be traveling with us, so it would be a plus if there was a separate area for them to be safe while traveling," Dot said.

The salesman nodded as he listened to the wish list, dollar signs replacing his pupils.

"How do you ladies plan to get around the areas while your RV is stationary?"

I looked at Dot. "Uh, we hadn't thought about that."

"Can you pull a car behind one of these?" Dot asked. "I suppose we could pull your car, Maisie." She looked at me questioningly.

"Absolutely," the salesman said. "But it does take some skill when you are pulling a tow. Have you thought about an Airstream?"

"A what?" I asked.

"Airstreams are very popular and one of our biggest sellers. They give you that vintage look with all the modern amenities. Once they are set up at the RV park, you would have access to your vehicle to get around the area. Do you have a vehicle with the power to tow?"

"I have a truck," Dot volunteered. "I used it to tow the moving trailer when I drove from Chicago to Florida. I think it would be adequate. Can we take a look at one?"

He led us to another lot, and I heard Dot gasp. My eyes must have been the size of saucers as we stood gawking at rows and rows of the classic, silver travel trailers. The rounded design and vintage look instantly stole our hearts. Some were cute as a bug, with room for no more than one. Others were as long as a big rig truck and looked like it could easily house a family of six.

"Can we see that one?" Dot pointed to what looked to be a medium-sized model.

He opened the door, and it was love at first sight. While I eyed the chef's kitchen, Dot checked out the fireplace and 50" flat screen tv and let out a sigh of pure pleasure. We looked at each other and knew without a word that this was it. After some negotiating, we were pleased with the cash discount and finally agreed on a sale price.

BACK IN THE CAR, I let out a squeal, barely able to contain my excitement. "I can't believe we just bought a travel trailer!" I said, bouncing up and down in the driver's seat.

Dot smiled from ear to ear. "I can't wait to decide where we'll go on our first road trip! I think we should each write down the places on our bucket list and put them all in a basket and draw one out. After the first one, we can take turns visiting the sites on our list. How does that sound?"

"That's a great idea," I agreed as I made the turn onto the highway and headed back to Palm Gardens. "Are you sure you're comfortable with pulling that thing?"

"I know I can do it. It'll just take some practice," Dot said. "After I take the truck and pick it up, I'll take it for several test runs in different situations and tight spots before we go on our first trip. That way I'll be more comfortable parking it and hooking it up."

I drove through the gated entrance to Palm Gardens and pulled to a stop in front of Dot's house. "I think we should meet at Avellino's for Italian tonight to celebrate."

"I've not eaten there yet, but it sounds delicious! See you there at 7:00 and bring your vacation ideas for our first big decision!" Dot said.

As soon as I walked in the house, I immediately pulled out my phone and called Fiona.

"Hello, Fiona!" I said when she answered. "I was thinking of having a little surprise get-together tonight at 6:45 at Avellino's to thank Dot for solving the case and taking down Mason's killer. Do you think you and Stanley might be able to come?"

"What a wonderful idea! Stanley is here right now and he's already nodding his head in agreement! We'll see you there!"

Next, I called Connie. She and Brad were excited to join us for dinner. She'd spent the morning with Officer Stone, signing her statement in the charges against Emily. Emily had turned herself in and confessed to helping Mason in his schemes at all three places of employment. She even admitted to taking the picture of George and the blonde.

Pete and Luther, always up for a good time and good food, would be there too. Everyone was looking forward to a delicious meal and a night out with friends. It would be a welcome diversion from the stress of the last week. I made sure they all knew to be on time, so we would all be there waiting when Dot arrived as the guest of honor.

AVELLINO'S WAS MY FAVORITE restaurant in Palm Grove. It wasn't fancy, but it was warm and inviting and the smell of garlic and oregano always took me back to Italian Nights at the restaurant. One night a month, Eddie and I would turn the place into an Italian eatery complete with checkered tablecloths and drippy candles in the center of each table. Eddie changed the music from the usual country to Rat Pack oldies and songs by old crooners like Frank Sinatra and Dean Martin. When I walked in, I saw the rest of the group gathered at a large table in the back. I had called my friend, Maria who worked as a server there, to reserve us a nice spot.

I saw Dot walk past the front window and open the door to the restaurant. She scanned the room until she caught sight of all of us and a smile spread across her face. As she made her way through the maze of tables to the back, Stanley began clapping. The rest of us joined in and soon the entire restaurant was cheering and applauding the local hero.

"What is this?" she exclaimed, her face three shades of red.

"It's just our way of saying thank you for caring about your friends enough to step out of retirement and bring a killer to justice. In fact, the whole town thanks you! Mr. Avellino said the entire party is on the house!"

"What do you think of my favorite place?" I asked after she'd had time to peruse the menu. "This crusty rosemary bread is to die for." I dipped a chunk into some herbed olive oil and popped it into my mouth.

"It's absolutely perfect. It smells like home," she said, fighting back tears.

After getting the group's attention, I told them the news of my and Dot's new plan for adventure. The gasps and chatter told me they were almost as excited as we were.

Maria took everyone's drink orders and I turned back to Dot. "So, no second thoughts?"

"No way! I'm ready to go!" Dot said excitedly. "Did you bring your list?"

I nodded as I pulled an envelope from my purse. "I even cut the places apart and folded them so we could draw one out. Do you have yours?"

"Here they are," Dot said pulling out a similar envelope. "I cut mine too!"

I took the envelopes, combined the contents into one and mixed them as much as I could while all our friends looked on.

Maria returned with our drinks and distributed them around the table.

"Maria, could you do us a big favor?" I smiled up at her. "Could you put your hand in this envelope and draw out one slip of paper?"

Maria laughed. "Sure. What am I pulling out? The name of your next husband?"

"My stars, no!" I laughed. "This, my friend, is the next big adventure." I shook the envelope one last time and handed it to Maria.

She reached in, pulled out a single slip of paper and handed it to Dot.

Dot closed her eyes and slowly unfolded the paper. She opened her eyes and read, "Nashville, Tennessee!"

"Music City, here we come!"

THE END

THE BUCKET LIST MYSTERIES are coming your way!!

Join Maisie, Dot and the pups on their first big road trip and send you Greetings from Nashville, Tennessee in *Boot Scootin' Bump Off*! Coming soon!

If you enjoyed *Dead in the Water*, please leave a review! It's very important to the success of an author! You can do that on Amazon, Goodreads, or wherever you like!

RECIPES

EASY 6-INGREDIENT BEEF & RICE CASSEROLE

SKILL LEVEL: EASY SERVES: 4-6

Ingredients

1 lb ground beef

½ medium onion, chopped

1 cup instant rice

1 can cream of chicken soup

1 can cream of mushroom soup

¼ cup Carnation Evaporated Milk

Instructions

Preheat oven to 350°

Brown ground beef in skillet with onion.

Drain off excess grease

Mix soup, meat, onion, rice and milk together in a 9"x9" baking dish

Bake for 50 minutes (or until bubbly and crunchy around the edges)

GRILLED SALMON WITH SUMMER VEGETABLES

SKILL LEVEL: EASY SERVES: 4

Ingredients

4 fresh salmon filets (4-6 oz ea)

4 Tbsp butter

1 tsp minced garlic

2 tsp minced fresh thyme

2 tsp minds fresh parsley

2 tsp lemon zest

Salt and pepper to taste

Lemon slices

Fresh vegetables of your choice (we like summer squash, zucchini, whole green beans, asparagus and small new potatoes)

Instructions

Preheat grill to medium heat (or oven to 400°)

Coat 4 large squares of heavy-duty foil with cooking spray

Cut all veggies into bite-sized pieces.

Arrange salmon and all veggies in the center of foil squares.

In a small bowl, mix together butter, garlic, thyme, parsley, lemon zest.

Season the filets with salt and pepper to taste.

Drop spoonfuls of the butter mixture over the salmon and veggies.

Fold over foil to seal packets tightly. Bake or grill for 15 minutes or until salmon is cooked through and vegetables are tender. Garnish with lemon slices.

Open packets carefully. If you feel salmon needs to cook a little longer, set open grill packets back on grill for another few minutes.

*Salmon is done when opaque in color and flakes easily. Do not overcook as it can be tough and dry.

*Recipe from www.dinneratthezoo.com

ALSO BY S.C. MERRITT

SWEETWATER SPRINGS Southern Mystery Series
Sideburns and Suspicions (Prequel Novella) FREE when you join my monthly CozyLetter!
Potluck and Pandemonium (Book 1)
Lakefronts and Larceny (Book 2)
Reunions and Reckonings (Book 3)
Moonshine and Murder (Book 4)
Fruitcakes and Fatalities (Book 5)
Cake and Corruption (Book 6)

OTHER SHORT STORIES
Caramelized Casualty (Christmas Cookie Cozies Anthology)

Killer Vacation (For Pet's Sake Cozy Anthology)

About the Author

S.C. Merritt is a Cozy Mystery Author whose stories feature southern female sleuths, plots with a twist and a little sprinkle of romance. The Sweetwater Springs Southern Mystery Series is set in a small Alabama town full of quirky characters, delicious restaurants and lots of murder. Yummy recipes are included in each book!

The Bucket List Mysteries feature two retirees who embark on the road trip of a lifetime to mark destinations off their bucket lists, but can't seem to steer clear of murder!

When not writing, she is traveling, watching classic movies and tv shows or collecting flamingos. She lives in Georgia with her husband, Vic, and miniature Schnauzer, Izzy and dreams of living in a tropical locale someday.

Follow her on Facebook at: @scmerrittwrites
Follow her on Instagram at: @scmerrittauthor
Read more at www.scmerritt.com.

Made in United States
Orlando, FL
24 June 2024